Appropriate Your Spiritual Endowments

Dearest Friend Lynn,

7-14-05

appropriate all god
has created you for!

Eph 4:13

Betty Nash Stuart

Betty Nash Stuart

xulon
PRESS

Xulon Press
11350 Random Hills Road
Suite 800
Fairfax, VA 22030
(703) 279-6511
XulonPress.com

To order additional copies,
call 1-866-909-BOOK (2665).

Scripture Theme

∞

But as it is written:
"Eye has not seen, nor ear heard,
Nor have entered into the heart of man
The things which God has prepared for those
who love Him."

*But God **has revealed them to us** through*
His Spirit.
For the Spirit searches all things, yes, the deep
things of God.
For what man knows the things of a man except
the spirit of the man which is in him?
Even so no one knows the things of God except the
Spirit of God.
Now we have received, not the spirit of the world,
but the Spirit who is from God,
***that we might know** the things that have been*
freely given to us by God.

These things we also speak, not in words which
man's wisdom teaches
but which the Holy Spirit teaches, comparing
spiritual things with spiritual.
But the natural man does not receive the things of
the Spirit of God,

for they are foolishness to him;
nor can he know them,
because they are spiritually discerned.
But he who is spiritual judges all things,
yet he himself is rightly judged by no one.
*For "who has known **the mind of the Lord** that he*
may instruct Him?"
But we have the mind of Christ.
(I Corinthians 2:9–16)

Dedication

∞

This is dedicated to all who desire to follow God's only begotten son, Jesus Christ. First of all, I lovingly submit this to my family members, sharing what I have gleaned from the Holy Scriptures and from walking with other believers in Jesus Christ as my Savior and Lord for many years. They know I'm not perfect, but according to God's Word, I am forgiven. I am encouraged to keep looking at His beloved pattern, His Son, Jesus, the author and finisher of our faith, according to Hebrews 12:2.

This is also dedicated to many friends I have enjoyed over the years who I want to see in eternity. Many of them are members of Aglow International, a blessed Christian women's ministry. They have taught me so many valuable treasures.

A writing acquaintance read some of this manuscript and said it was too deep. If it reads that way, it is because I wasted too many years as a surface Christian. This book is meant to motivate readers to go deep in the Lord and His service to their unique world. This is where the abundant life in Christ is to be found.

—*Betty Nash Stuart*

Table of Contents

∞

Introduction

∞

There can be no significant spiritual growth for believers in Jesus Christ apart from partaking of the Word of God. It must gain access to both our souls and our spirits. By regularly reading from the Old and New Testaments of the Bible, we come to understand God's will personally. Jeremiah recorded these words from God to believers ages ago: "You will seek Me and find Me, when you search for Me with all your heart" (Jeremiah 29:13).

Jesus said, "If you abide in My word, you are My disciples indeed" (John 8:31). This is a vital requirement for our ongoing progression into the mature, overcoming Christian life.

Ask Christians who take quality time to study and memorize Bible portions if it makes a difference in the quality of their lives. Without exception, you will get positive responses. They will readily attest to the rich blessings and invaluable personal guidance they receive. Studying God's Word is one of the joyful disciplines in life that brings life-changing benefits.

Believers who store Scripture verses in their minds and hearts relate that they experience new dimensions of peace and faith. They become aware of God's guidance and discernment about life's circumstances. It produces unshakable stability. By memorizing and meditating on biblical commandments, principles, and promises, these believers are able to progress from a mere belief in an unapproachable God to fully trusting their heavenly Father's loving care and concern through these life-changing instructions.

Jesus Christ becomes a reality, not just a divine historical figure. He becomes our personal Savior and then, progressively, the Lord of our lives. We come to know and enjoy His abiding companionship through the Holy Spirit. This can happen only when we feed on the true Bread of Heaven, which Jesus declared that He is. The "Word of God" is one of repeated New Testament titles of Jesus Christ.

When the dynamic truths of God's laws and commandments are understood, we are challenged to grow in spirit and in truth. Our daily circumstances become practical opportunities for God's Spirit to help us meet these situations in a scriptural and victorious way. This growth process causes Christ to be formed in us, as stated in Galatians 4:19.

We are being molded by the Master Potter. Being born again means radical change! But just as the expansion of any object brings stress, so we must be willing and embrace stress so changes will occur. Our heavenly Father has a unique destiny for each one of us that His Holy Spirit is grooming us to fill.

In the parable of the sower in Luke 8, Jesus taught that all who are unwilling to experience spiritual growth soon fall by the wayside. The primary cause is the lack of nourishment required for spiritual growth. Only God's Word can feed our spiritual lives. How much wiser to be motivated and changed by God's instruction book rather than in "the school of hard knocks." His magnificent promises assure us that He intends to conform us into the image of Jesus, His firstborn Son. Awesome, but true. Jesus is the pattern Son (see Romans 8:14, 29).

As we prayerfully consider the thirty-one topics in this meditation, we will more fully comprehend the fact that we are on a spiritual journey toward sonship. None of us have arrived yet, but we all have a glorious eternal destiny ahead. It includes the opportunity of reigning with King Jesus in positions of responsibility. Our heavenly Father can reserve His assignments only for those who are matured through obedience. Let us hunger to attain that destiny.

The admonition of Colossians 3:16 states, "Let the word of Christ dwell in you richly in all wisdom." This is a clarion call to go beyond just reading the Bible casually. Clergy and laymen alike are meant to be ambassadors for Christ, growing in knowledge of the wisdom and purposes of God for fruitful service, both now and later. It is our on-the-job training for eternal positions of kingdom responsibility.

Father God, through His gift of grace, enables us to understand and have a continuing desire for His written Word. But as we learn from the parable of the sower, He knows that there will also be some who are exposed to His truth and will treat it carelessly or neglect it altogether.

The only way to become an overcoming believer who will reap the rich promises in the book of Revelation (see chapters 2 and 3) is by learning and applying God's spiritual laws and principles. They cannot be excluded or circumvented on our part. This is His specific will for every regenerated child of God.

This is the purpose of this devotional meditation of thirty-one chapters. As we determine to commit ourselves to feed daily on the life-changing Scriptures, we can be assured that we will not only be instructed and inspired, but also corrected whenever our feet stray outside the path to eternal glory. May we all continue to be challenged to become appropriators of all the rich endowments, provisions, and promises that the Holy Scriptures contain. God's Holy Spirit will illuminate our understanding of our present and future potentials in Christ as we claim and apply the powerful truths of the Bible's timeless message.

* * * * *

Prayer:

Dear Heavenly Father: I come to You now, in the precious name of Jesus, and say that I want to make a fresh commitment to faithfully feed on Your Word daily, that I may be pleasing in Your sight and usable for Your purposes. Give me a renewed hunger for and an understanding of Your truth. Amen.

CHAPTER 1

Appropriate God's Salvation

∞

And this is the testimony: that God has given us
eternal life, and this life is in His Son.
(I John 5:11)

There is an amazing truth about God's salvation that is still obscured from the multitudes. Yet when known and appropriated, it has the power to dramatically change lives. This powerful truth is able to set captives free, even those who have lived behind political iron and bamboo curtains or inside prison walls.

However, in every generation for twenty centuries, a growing company of people has grasped this life-changing truth. They make up the expanding fellowship of true believers in Jesus Christ worldwide who have become appropriators of the eternal benefits of the New Testament's gospel message.

The truth is that God's salvation is already every man's portion, bought and paid for by the shed blood of Jesus Christ on Calvary's cross. We can't earn it or buy it. We can only by faith appropriate it, and then confess it as ours (see I John 2:2).

This is the true gospel of the kingdom of God. Jesus Christ commissioned His first disciples to proclaim it to all nations. What they preached is recorded as the Apostle Peter's very first sermon: "Repent, and let every one of you be baptized in the name of Jesus Christ for the remission of sins; and you shall receive the gift of the Holy Spirit" (Acts 2:38).

Why is it that in any generation, those who truly receive the person of Jesus Christ as their personal Savior through repentance have always been a minority? Primarily, the majority of mankind remains unaware of what their Creator has said about accepting His genuine salvation. Satan, the enemy of our souls, strives to keep us as the ignorant citizens of his kingdom of darkness. This is a kingdom of sin and death. Through Adam's disobedience, all of mankind is born into this domain of darkness.

We can find the reference to two distinct kingdom realms in Colossians 1:12–14: "Giving thanks to the Father who has qualified us to be partakers of the inheritance of the saints in the light. He has delivered us from the power of darkness and conveyed us into the kingdom of the Son of His love, in whom we have redemption through His blood, the forgiveness of sins."

Although some may dispute the present-day reality of a stronghold of spiritual darkness, this reality can be plainly read in God's record, the Bible. Many people are unwilling to acknowledge that God has said that their sins call for repentance. They are trying to save themselves with their own futile efforts. They are holding delusions of security with a false self-righteousness. Unknowingly, Satan has sold them his biggest lie.

Claims have always been made of many methods to reach God, or of all religions being basically the same. Some foolishly teach that man can become his own savior through self-betterment or good works. But this is the divine declaration we find in both the Old and New Testaments: "Truly, in vain is salvation hoped for from the hills, and from the multitude of mountains; truly, in the Lord our God is the salvation of Israel" (Jeremiah 3:23). Again, the Apostle Peter preached about Jesus Christ in Acts 4:12: "Nor is there salvation in any other, for there is no other name under heaven given among men by which we must be saved."

The fact is that some have come to true salvation by hearing the gospel message of John 3:16, that God gave His only begotten Son, Jesus, and that whoever believes in Him would not perish, but have everlasting life. But sadly, later in their lives, they come to doubt their spiritual condition. Needlessly they spend hours, days, or even years filled with uncertainty of their salvation. This happens because they are not reading their Bibles. Only by feeding on and understanding God's Word can their doubts be eliminated.

Where do you stand? Are you living in the "rest" that is promised to those who do not doubt God's Word? Or are you one who wavers back and forth without that blessed assurance of being a redeemed child of God? Chapters three and four of the book of Hebrews clearly present both positions. One is of doubt, disobedience, and rejection. The other is of faith mixed with obedience, bringing a blessed rest of the soul and peace with God.

The good news is that believers don't have to fall into this dead end. The key to victorious living is in putting our complete trust in God. Throughout the Bible, God is shown to be calling for His people to listen to Him. We must abide by His recorded words of truth to develop our spiritual hearing. Only in this way will we be firmly secure in our eternal relationship and destiny. Satan, setbacks, or circumstances cannot move us.

For those who waver in faith, their paths are filled with doubt, instability, and even despair. By failing to seek out and believe the promises in God's Word, they are usually erratic in their attempts to learn how to read their spiritual roadmap, the Bible. Ignorance of their rightful position in Christ makes them easy targets for their enemies, Satan and his minions, whose roles are to harass, rob, and destroy.

In today's language, a "yo-yo Christian" well describes the up-and-down emotional life of a person who is in bondage of uncertainty. This is not only unfruitful and stressful, but it short-circuits any spiritual growth. Think how this grieves the heart of God.

Our heavenly Father has made provision, through the gift of faith, for all believers to walk in liberty, trust, and peace. But we all must activate that faith by believing that true salvation is ours in Jesus Christ.

The gospel record states that God's redemptive plan provided His Son as every person's Redeemer. The shed blood of Jesus Christ is full payment, or complete atonement, for the sin debt of all mankind. God's Holy Spirit not only initiated the written Word, but He also has the ability to help us believe the fact that we have received reconciliation to God the Father.

Throughout these daily meditations, the focus is on the many provisions of God for our spiritual birth and growth to maturity. But we are all responsible to appropriate these provisions and to incorporate them into our lives. The purpose is to challenge each reader to give daily priority to studying a portion of Scripture.

There are no shortcuts to spiritual maturity. It is a lifetime journey for which we must obtain continual nourishment, wisdom, and strength to overcome life's circumstances. This will come as we daily study the Scriptures and fellowship with God the Father, His Son Jesus, and the Holy Spirit. We also need to have the protective covering of pastors and fellowship with other believers to whom we can be accountable. When we live in this intimate relationship, we will experience the double promise of the love and the abiding presence of the Godhead, as portrayed in John 14:21–23. These verses contain awesome promises that are meant for every believer. Take a moment to read these verses, and then let your mind and spirit also enjoy the impact of today's theme text, I John 5:11.

Consciously realize that this is indeed the pledged word of God to you personally. Eternal life is to be found only in His Son, Jesus Christ. Meditate on the promise that because you have come to repentance as one needing a Savior, and you have received

Him, you also have this eternal life resident in you now.

* * * * *

Prayer:

Dear Heavenly Father: I come to You in Jesus' name. I am thankful that His precious blood was shed for me, and has made me an eternal part of the family of God. I confess this day that I need and desire Jesus as my Savior and Lord of my life. Help me grow in the knowledge that I need to become a mature Christian. Amen.

CHAPTER 2

Appropriate Forgiveness

∽

If we confess our sins, He is faithful and just to
forgive us our sins and to cleanse us from all
unrighteousness.
(I John 1:9)

To appropriate God's forgiveness is to enter into God's peace. The inability to totally understand this forgiveness can be the prime cause of much anguish in the Christian's life. When a believer does not fully comprehend and apply this major spiritual grace to his life, he will continue to suffer needlessly with recurring guilt.

The basic principle of the Christian faith has two equally important aspects: first, God's total forgiveness expressed toward all who will come under the atonement purchased by Jesus Christ; and second, our forgiveness toward others. Any failure to incorporate the full, freeing truth of this two-part application throws a roadblock in the path of our spiritual growth.

Today's text is a promise that was fully purchased for us by the shed blood of Jesus Christ. He ably met God's conditions for the forgiveness of mankind's sins at Calvary. His Holy Spirit also provides us with sufficient faith to believe and to receive full pardon. When we do, we find true rest for our souls. We have peace with God.

Whenever we recognize sin in our lives, we are to confess that sin to our heavenly Father, and as our text verse states, He will forgive us. As we stay sensitive to God's Word and His Spirit, we will have the ability to recognize when we need to do this.

The book of Colossians opens with the Apostle Paul giving a brief review of the gospel. The text says that he prayed for believers who have faith in Jesus Christ and who know the grace of God in truth, that they would be filled with the knowledge of God's will in all wisdom and spiritual understanding (Colossians 1:3–9). This would include the important principle of forgiveness.

Paul states in verse fourteen that believers have redemption through Christ's blood, which means the forgiveness of our sins. Understanding this truth brings peace that nothing can disturb. We have then truly appropriated God's forgiveness.

When this occurs, we enter into the rich father-and-child relationship that was prepared for us before the foundation of the world. Our heavenly Father, the Creator of the universe, knew that for His unrestricted work to begin in our transformation, we must have His peace activated in our minds, souls, and spirits.

The second distinct part of appropriating forgiveness is for us to activate it in our human relationships. What is God's strong word on this matter? It is recorded in Mark 11:25–26: "And whenever you stand praying, if you have anything against anyone, forgive him, that your Father in heaven may also forgive you your trespasses. But if you do not forgive, neither will your Father in heaven forgive your trespasses." This commandment should cause us to understand the seriousness of any unforgiveness in our lives. The fact is that we actually block God's forgiveness to us while we are withholding it from others. This attitude causes a break in our fellowship with God, but not in our relationship to Him. We are still His children, but we are in rebellion to His vital commandment.

Because God hates sin, but not the sinner, He will not and cannot permit us to embrace a condition that blocks our spiritual growth. He allows us to come to a static place in our Christian experience that is meant to trigger our attention. God's Spirit is quenched and grieved by unforgiveness. One may be ignorant of the source of this condition, but will have a sense of unrest and a lack of peace and joy. (God's Spirit brings conviction, but He doesn't condemn.) It is one of the imperative reasons that Christians must learn what the Bible has to teach us about this essential principle.

Learning to function in the grace of forgiveness in all of our relationships is a freeing factor for walking in peace. As we think back to times when forgiveness was needed, we usually remember that those situations robbed our peace, as well as our mental and even physical energy. We experience stress when we try to place the blame on those who have wronged us instead of simply obeying the command to forgive. We need to realize that God is fully able to deal with the others involved if we will let go of the matters.

The statement in Ephesians 4:32 has the stimulus to dissolve our resistance to be forgiving: "And be kind to one another, tenderhearted, forgiving one another, even as God in Christ forgave you." Doesn't that disarm your resentments?

Sometimes the unforgiveness we hold is toward God! This can be an unconscious and even a long-standing condition. An untimely death of a loved one, a deep disappointment, or an unfair circumstance can be the source of holding God to blame. Bringing this to light often produces breakthroughs in Christian counseling.

By focusing on the Scriptures mentioned earlier, we can come to grips with releasing this unforgiveness in sincere prayers of repentance. We understand that God's mercy and readiness to receive our confessions will bring healing restoration.

It is important to speak of the real healings that can occur through our acts of forgiving. Holding on to unforgiveness and experiencing physical or emotional illness as a result is a recognized fact. Both the religious community and the medical world have given this proven phenomenon well-deserved study.

In some cases, conditions such as ulcers, arthritic disturbances, or chronic asthma have gone into complete remission as those afflicted have heeded instructions to let go of long-standing grudges, resentments, or disappointments through acts of forgiveness.

Even when we feel unable to bring ourselves to the act and expression of forgiving, there is a way. By prayerfully asking God to make us *willing* to forgive, we open the way for this miracle to take place in our hearts. It is the grace and mercy of God in action! It is beyond our understanding, and can only be experienced and enjoyed. Isn't it a blessing to realize that He works with our sometimes negative, hindering human conditions?

* * * * *

Prayer:

Father God, in Jesus' name, I thank You that He died for the forgiving atonement of all my sins. I thank You that You are so willing to forgive and cleanse me when I ask. Please keep me sensitive to Your Holy Spirit and Your Word, that I may always keep short accounts with You. Amen.

CHAPTER 3

Appropriate the Baptism in the Holy Spirit

∽

I indeed baptize you with water unto repentance,
but He who is coming after me is mightier than I,
whose sandals I am not worthy to carry.
He will baptize you with the Holy Spirit and fire.
(Matthew 3:11)

Do you have witnessing power in your life? Do you feel as though you are making progress in the overcoming Christian life? If you can't answer in the positive, have you expressly asked Jesus to baptize you with His Holy Spirit? Maybe you are like the believers recorded in Acts who replied when asked if they had received the Holy Spirit when they believed: "We have not so much as heard whether there is a Holy Spirit" (Acts 19:2).

Although Jesus was born of Mary, by the power of God's Holy Spirit (Luke 1:35), He did not begin

His earthly power ministry until after He was baptized by John (Luke 3:21–22). At that time, the gospel records that God the Father caused His Spirit to descend upon Jesus in a visible and audible manifestation and said, "You are My beloved Son; in You I am well pleased" (3:22). In the verse that follows, Luke states that Jesus' ministry immediately began.

The Luke account states that shortly afterwards, Jesus was in the synagogue and read from Isaiah 61, the prophetic declaration of His anointing to serve. Although the Holy Spirit was *with* Jesus from conception, He did no miracle until He was anointed by God's Spirit and had a release of the divine power flow in His life.

Today, under the New Testament's authority, every Spirit-baptized believer can speak forth the same Luke 4:18–19 testimony: "The Spirit of the Lord is upon Me, because He has anointed Me to preach the gospel to the poor; He has sent Me to heal the brokenhearted, to proclaim liberty to the captives and recovery of sight to the blind, to set at liberty those who are oppressed; to proclaim the acceptable year of the Lord."

If we could observe the present-day body of believers in any local fellowship, we would not yet see the majority walking in true anointing knowledge. In some groups, the people are not aware, nor have they received scriptural instruction about this vital anointing baptism for service, which is available to every true believer. Even in fellowships where the reality of the Holy Spirit's full ministry is known and taught, there is usually only a partial appropriation and participation of these "new birth" rights.

We are well aware of the reality of unfulfilled potential by the stunted growth of any living organism. The same result occurs when a sincere person comes to Jesus Christ in true repentance for salvation, and stops there. If he never surrenders to Jesus as the Lord of his life, he misses his true potential and effectiveness as a viable, functioning part of the body of Christ. His spiritual growth is less than it was meant to be.

The baptism we are speaking of here has many descriptive terms, including being baptized with, being filled with, or being emerged in the Holy Spirit. All of these terms are really describing the Lord's response to our full surrender to His lordship. Reverend Jack Hayford, a highly respected Christian pastor, author, and conference speaker, stated that although this baptism is furnished and made available to the believer at the time of salvation, we must actively partake of what has already been given. He likened it to the consummation of a marriage. And it surely is a more intimate relationship to know Jesus as Lord, rather than as only the Savior, even as important as that is.

Some may ask why it is necessary to receive this baptism. It really is not an option on our part. It is a command of God to all who come to Jesus for salvation. It is giving the Spirit of God unhindered freedom to live effectively through our lives to carry out His commission to evangelize our unique world. The Holy Spirit of God is the facilitator of the power of God!

Christians who have experienced this baptism in and of God's Spirit unanimously testify to very dramatic added dimensions in their lives. They see growing expressions in the fruit of the Spirit in themselves, beginning with love and joy, which they know are beyond their own capacity. That, in turn, increases their inspiration to worship, with an enlarged awareness of who God is and who they are in Him.

They report a new sense of God-given authority and compassionate power in prayer. They have a new level of understanding of the Bible message. This gives them the sensitivity to receive God's guidance, along with a heightened desire to serve others by cooperating with the Spirit of God in the manifestation of His gifts through them.

Jesus is the baptizer, as our theme text states. As He commissioned His first disciples, He also exhorted them to receive the Holy Spirit (John 20:22). We then need only to direct our expectant petition to Him in faith to receive what He is so very desiring to impart to His own followers.

A pastor or another believer may pray with you to receive, or you may be alone. As believers, we need to only be ready to receive. Let's build on the letters in the word "ready":

> R: *Repent* of any known sin in your life. Acts 2:38: "Repent, and let every one of you be baptized in the name of Jesus Christ for the remission of sins; and you shall receive the gift of the Holy Spirit."

> E: *Expect* to receive what Jesus promised.

Acts 1:8: "But you shall receive power when the Holy Spirit has come upon you; and you shall be witnesses to Me."

A: *Ask* in faith. Hebrews 11:6: "But without faith it is impossible to please Him, for he who comes to God must believe that He is, and that He is a rewarder of those who diligently seek Him."

D: *Drink,* or thirst after God's anointing. Matthew 5:6: "Blessed are those who hunger and thirst for righteousness, for they shall be filled."

Y: *Yield* fully to the lordship of Christ. I Corinthians 12:3b: "No one can say that Jesus is Lord except by the Holy Spirit."

* * * * *

Prayer:

Dear Father God: My desire is to receive all that You have for me. Just as I came to You empty-handed for salvation and received it, in the name of Jesus I now come, asking Him to be the Lord of my life and to baptize me in Your Holy Spirit. I am going to believe that I receive on the basis of Your words that I have just read. I thank You and praise You. Amen.

CHAPTER 4

Appropriate Wholeness for Your Spirit, Soul, and Body

∽

*Now may the God of peace Himself sanctify you
completely;
and may your whole spirit, soul, and body be
preserved blameless
at the coming of our Lord Jesus Christ.
(I Thessalonians 5:23)*

What a potential pronouncement! We believers thrill as we consider our future perfection when Jesus Christ returns. But how much of that completeness can we expect during our lifetimes? Can we expand our faith to appropriate a greater wholeness now in the three essential components of our beings: spirit, soul, and body?

Each of us is a soul, which comprises a mind, will, and emotions. As believers, we all now have spirits that have been quickened and regenerated by

God's Holy Spirit, who is His means of communication with us. These two unique features of the human species reside in our physical bodies, thus making us the three-part beings that our theme text portrays.

Let us seek the illumination of God's Spirit as we consider this powerful scriptural benediction to believers in Christ. Though this verse is to be totally fulfilled in the eternal future, at this present time we can each make a conscious decision to seek this quality of life now. We have the privilege to ask God for what is repeatedly promised to believers in both the Old and New Testaments.

Some religions erroneously teach that there is no sickness or sin, which is a matter of wrong thinking and is opposed to God's Word. He states that there is sickness and there will be sin operating in mankind. But we can also read that He has provided our deliverance from both conditions. How can we realistically deny the fact that disease does exist? We do at times experience physical or emotional illnesses, not to mention injuries. But if we are to believe God's position on the matter, we don't have to remain afflicted. His Word tells us to seek both complete healing and the loosing of sin's bondage by looking to our source, Jesus Christ.

In the Old Testament, the book of Proverbs is overflowing with distinct promises that are meant to bring wholeness. It is very rewarding to review these thirty-one chapters often. One's understanding can be considerably deepened by a studied reading of these divine exhortations, using various Bible versions for added understanding.

"If you will turn (repent) and give heed to my

reproof, behold, I [Wisdom] will pour out my spirit upon you, I will make my words known to you" (Proverbs 1:23). Our spirits and souls are the beneficiaries here. And again in 3:21–22: "Keep sound and godly Wisdom and discretion, and they will be life to your inner self, and a gracious ornament to your neck (your outer self)" (Amplified Bible).

The counsel for physical wholeness is found in Proverbs 3:7–8 (Amplified Bible): "Be not wise in your own eyes; reverently fear and worship the Lord and turn [entirely] away from evil. It shall be health to your nerves and sinews, and marrow and moistening to your bones."

What a testimony and rich assurance that our heavenly Father is concerned about His children's wholeness! The Bible should be our primary health book. Who knows our needs better than our Creator?

In discovering the many pertinent Scriptures that are related to a believer's wellbeing, several underlying keys repeatedly surface. They involve the cause-and-effect principle. These keys, or spiritual principles, all have to do with our obedience to God's established rules for living. Take time to read Psalm 107 for a full disclosure of our responsibilities and God's response to our actions.

This obedience is in regard to our relationship to Him, to our fellowmen, and to ourselves. A good example is recorded in Luke 17:11–19, which is the account of ten lepers who came to Jesus for mercy and healing. In addressing Jesus as Master, they show not only a willingness to be obedient, but also their faith in His ability to heal.

Jesus gave them a direct command: "Go, show

yourselves to the priests" (verse 14). This was the customary way to receive documentation of a contagious disease being healed so a person could be reinstated into the community. All ten lepers started toward the temple, and God's mercy was manifest. It is stated that "as they went, they were cleansed." Their instant obedience brought immediate results!

As the account continues, a second key for wholeness is revealed: the key of thanksgiving and praise. Luke, who was a doctor, records that of the ten lepers who were cleansed, only one vocally glorified God. He also gave public thanksgiving by praising the healing Jesus. It was at this specific point that Jesus declared, "Your faith has made you well" (verse 19). In the original Greek text, this is rendered, "Thy faith has saved thee." It is interesting to know that the word *salvation* in the Greek language encompasses the meaning of *wholeness.*

Remember that first there is the record of cleansing of the leprosy, then a condition of wholeness is declared. One could easily assume that Jesus was merely stating that a man's physical body had received healing. But there is an additional possibility to consider. Because of this one leper's attitude and actions of thanksgiving and praise, Jesus may well have been announcing a wholeness of the man's spirit and soul as well, which the other nine missed.

We have looked at our relationship to God in the two keys above. The third key that we must apply for optimum wholeness is in our human relationships, specifically in forgiveness. As we discussed in chapter two, while we are operating in a state of unforgiven sin, which is disobedience to God's law, our wholeness is eroded. We established by Scriptures that forgiveness is to be expressed when needed between man and God as well as in all of our human relationships.

It is imperative that we keep short accounts with God according to His scriptural commandments through confession and true repentance (Mark 11:25–26). One of the distinct benefits of the ordinance of Holy Communion is that of examining our past conduct to see if we need to ask for forgiveness or to extend it to others.

Read what I Corinthians 11:28–31 states about taking Communion in a correct manner: "But let a man examine himself, and so let him eat of that bread and drink of the cup. For he who eats and drinks in an unworthy manner eats and drinks judgment to himself, not discerning the Lord's body. For this reason many are weak and sick among you, and many sleep. For if we would judge ourselves, we would not be judged."

We believers in Jesus Christ can expect to walk in an increased degree of wholeness as we follow these biblical keys of obedience, thanksgiving, praise, and forgiveness.

* * * * *

Prayer:

Dear Father God: In the name of Jesus I thank You that Your Word is indeed both living and powerful, sharper than any two-edged sword, piercing even to the division of my soul and spirit, and of my joints and marrow, and is a discerner of the thoughts and intents of my heart.[1]* Make me to desire Your truth in my inward parts, that I may walk in wholeness and give glory to You as my source. Amen.

CHAPTER 5

Appropriate the Divine Presence

∞

Jesus answered and said to him,
"If anyone loves Me, he will keep My word;
and My Father will love him, and We will come to
him and make Our home with him."
(John 14:23)

Although we cannot totally comprehend the full reality of this thrilling promise, we can still let this precious truth take root deep within our souls and spirits. This is the priceless availability of the continual abiding companionship with the Divinity. In faith let us appropriate this divine presence offered to every believer. Receiving the mighty revelation of this heavenly fellowship will change and enhance the very quality of our daily lives.

This astounding pledge should cause our souls and spirits to leap every time we read or consider it. The fact that we mortals can experience this supreme

relationship is not always given adequate consideration. How lavish we should be in our daily thanksgiving and praise for this amazing offer. It is
something so awesome in quality that the world cannot relate to it. Any mention of "talking to God"
often brings scoffing, and the speaker is immediately
classified politely as a mystic or just downright
crazy.

As with so many of God's promises, this one is
repeated numerous times throughout the Scriptures.
Revelation 3:20 states, "Behold, I stand at the door
and knock. If anyone hears My voice and opens the
door, I will come in to him and dine with him, and
he with Me." Again we have the intimate invitation
of fellowship.

How patient and persistent is our God. So often
we let the cares and activities of our world rob us of
the most needful relationship available. He is the
source of all of our dearest needs. In fact, for the professing Christian who does not appropriate this
unique spiritual intercourse, he has settled for only a
religion, and is not fully partaking of the intended
life-giving communion. He is settling for a stunted
and unstable Christian life, a barren religious experience containing little real joy.

Andrew Murray, a beloved and insightful nine-
teenth-century Christian author, wrote about this true
and progressive discipleship: "First following, then
knowing the Lord. The believing surrender to Jesus
and the surrender to His Word to expect what
appears most improbable is the only way to the full
blessedness of knowing Him" (*Abide in Christ,*
Christian Literature Crusade Publishers).

Today we are living in a world of more than five billion people. God's Word tells us that He loves and is concerned for each one. For the true believer in Jesus Christ, God has the capacity and the desire to make Himself available through this abiding presence of His triune being. Realizing that our finite minds are incapable of really grasping the depths of this relationship, He has graciously supplied each of us with the faith necessary to receive.

As we accept and welcome this dazzling possibility, we find an increasing ability to enjoy His reality in our lives. Three prime areas are open to us: a deeper understanding of the Scriptures, God's peace, and answered prayer.

The primary area that validates this relationship is the Word of God. Instead of merely reading a historical account of God's dealings with humanity, the Word begins to "speak" to us personally. As we study the Scriptures, we uncover answers to many spiritual and human questions we have had. Even directions for our daily lives are given as we pursue the knowledge of God's will through His written Word.

Jesus claims His lordship over those who sincerely read the Bible with a love for Him as Savior. His Holy Spirit plants the life of Christ within readers with Scripture seed. The fruit of the Spirit grows in us as we act in obedience to the commandments and spiritual principles to be found in the Word of God. We are making Him Lord of our lives.

When we fellowship with God daily, we walk in peace. We come to realize that our Creator truly is in charge. Understanding that we are beloved children of God, we learn to trust in our heavenly Father's care, in good times and bad. The twenty-third Psalm becomes our personal birthright. We say with new understanding, "The Lord *is* my shepherd; I shall not want."

Thirdly, as new believers see prayers being answered, they have proof that indeed they are now part of a relationship with power. Jesus promises that if we will abide in Him, and His Word abides in us, we will see answered prayers (see John 15:7). God's Spirit will impress us to pray for the needs of others. As we see changes in their circumstances, it further assures us that we are part of a valid, benevolent partnership. God is working His love into our hearts through compassionate intercessory prayer. Prayer is a powerful spiritual endowment that we will continue to cover in this devotional.

"Lo, I am with you always, even to the end of the age" (Matthew 28:20) is a familiar phrase of the divine presence to every believer. We would not consciously shun or ignore this glorious gift, but let us each ponder just how consistent is our daily appropriation of this divine nurturing love and fellowship that is so freely offered. May this precious blessing of God's pledge to abide go deep into our souls and spirits as we meditate on His Word.

* * * * *

Prayer:
Dear Father God: Although I cannot understand how You would make Yourself available to mortal man, I have confidence in Your promises that it is so.

Just as You communed with Adam and Eve, and with Your people throughout history, I am so thankful that Your Spirit is my comforting holy companion. In Jesus' name, I praise You. Amen.

CHAPTER 6

Appropriate Your New Covenant

∞

How much more shall the blood of Christ,
who through the eternal Spirit offered Himself
without spot to God,
cleanse your conscience from dead works
to serve the living God?
And for this reason He is the Mediator of
the new covenant,
by means of death, for the redemption of the
transgressions under the first covenant,
that those who are called may receive the promise
of the eternal inheritance.
(Hebrews 9:14–15)

It has been said that if you don't know what you have as a believer in Jesus Christ, read your contract. A contract or covenant is defined as an agreement between two or more parties for doing, or not doing, something specific. Hence, the New Testament is God's new covenant or contract with us.

The epistle to the Hebrews has been called the greatest book on Christ and theology. It is also aptly termed the "Book of Better Things," as the expression "better" is used or specifically implied numerous times. The message was written to Hebrew Christians who wanted to return to the religious bondage of Judaism. The epistle to the Galatians centers on correcting the same error, that of religious practices rather than relationship, and may have been written at the same time.

A major component of this new covenant informs us of the promised rest of God spoken of in Hebrews 4:9–10: "There remains therefore a rest for the people of God. For he who has entered His rest has himself also ceased from his works as God did from His." This verse is not to imply we are to lie down on the job of being Christ's witnesses to our world, but it refers to that of working to gain our salvation.

God not only instigated this new covenant, but His Son fulfilled the requirements on Calvary's cross. We enter in through our faith, and by the grace of God. Then we are to "work out our salvation" by being obedient and fruitful (see Philippians 2:12).

As we study the features of this better covenant, established on better promises, we learn just what Jesus Christ, our Great High Priest, has accomplished on our behalf. No other book of the New Testament, apart from the four Gospels, so clearly conveys the selflessness of our Savior's atoning sacrifice. We come to understand that it was through much testing, suffering, and the shedding of His own blood unto death that He became the author of eternal salvation of all who will personally receive and follow Him.

We are assured that Jesus is not only able to compassionately understand our weaknesses, but that He was in all points tempted as we are, yet without sin (Hebrews 4:15). That allows each one of us to come to our heavenly Father in an open, paternal relationship, knowing that He never wants to condemn us when we do sin. He is only interested in bringing us to a conviction of His displeasure and the harm we are imposing on ourselves and others. Listen to this plea: "Let us therefore come boldly to the throne of grace, that we may obtain mercy and find grace to help in time of need" (Hebrews 4:16).

We are told in this better covenant, inaugurated by a better, sinless priest, that while the Old Testament law made nothing perfect, we now have a better hope. We are reminded that the former commandments were ministered by mortal priests with weaknesses so they needed to offer up sacrifices for themselves as well as for the people. Now we place our hope in One who is holy, harmless, and undefiled, and through His better sacrifices has been perfected forever!

This minister of the true tabernacle states, "I will be merciful to their unrighteousness, and their sins and their lawless deeds I will remember no more" (Hebrews 8:12). These tremendous declarations should motivate our praise and unflagging thanksgiving. By these new covenant promises, we are the recipients of God's abundant mercy and grace. How can we possibly keep this good news to ourselves?

The Apostle Paul states that believers are called

to be able ministers of this new covenant, which he terms the ministry of the Spirit or the ministry of righteousness: "For if the ministry of condemnation[2*] had glory, the ministry of righteousness exceeds much more in glory" (II Corinthians 3:9).

* * * * *

Prayer:

Dear heavenly Father: In the name of Jesus, I thank You for all the benefits of Your new covenant. May I never lose sight of how much You love me, and the supreme price that was paid for my salvation. Burn these truths deep within my heart and soul, that my life will be a witness to Your blessed reality and great love. Amen.

CHAPTER 7

Appropriate Your Righteous Position

∞

For He made Him who knew no sin to be sin for us,
that we might become the righteousness of
God in Him.
(II Corinthians 5:21)

This theme text declares that on the cross, Jesus Christ established our position of righteousness with God before we ever believed in Him as our Savior and Lord. Yet how many earnest Christians, unaware of their purchased right standing with God, are enjoying this important aspect of their present position in the kingdom of God?

Although two thousand years have passed since the indescribable price was paid for our righteous position in Christ, most of Christendom still has not actually comprehended what Isaiah so clearly recorded: "And the effect of righteousness will be peace [internal and external], and the result of righteousness will be quietness and confident trust for-ever" (Isaiah 32:17, Amplified Bible).

The peace of God is to be the path of God's children in our daily walk. When our position of being in right standing with God is not a clear reality, the circumstances of life continually cause us much unrest. When we sin, we are often so appalled by feelings of self-condemnation that at times we forget to seek forgiveness. We neglect the avenue of repentance that is always open to us through the shed blood of our Lord. This robs us and the whole body of believers much valuable time and fruitfulness.

In the New Testament, believers are designated by various descriptive titles such as "heirs of God and joint heirs with Christ," "the temple of God's Holy Spirit," "Christ's ambassadors," "ministers of reconciliation," and "a chosen royal priesthood." All of these titles have been registered in God's kingdom for believers who have become the righteousness of God to serve Him.

In the United States of America, well over fifty percent of the people polled state they are of the Christian faith. Yet we do not see the expected moral influence that should result from this majority. In reality, we see sinful conditions blatantly in control in every sphere of American life. The news media bears testimony to this sad condition in business and political worlds, as well in all strata of our society. It is even to be found on both sides of the bench in our courts.

The good news is that this eroding moral decline can (and must) be challenged. The body of Christ has been a sleeping giant that holds biblical answers to humanity's sin problem. Too few of us are in the battle for righteousness. We can be aroused only by knowing who we are in Christ, and that we are responsible to God for what He has invested in each one of us.

Today's sincere Christians must become committed Christians. We need to remember that as partakers of God's Holy Word, we are being equipped to be His witnesses to our world of influence. We must assume the reality of that commission and appropriate our rightful position as ministers of reconciliation. Read about this more fully in II Corinthians 4. Paul's exhortation is highly motivating.

Here is what James writes: "But he who looks into the perfect law of liberty and continues in it, and is not a forgetful hearer but a doer of the work, this one will be blessed in what he does" (James 1:25). This principle is still an active divine promise today.

It doesn't require a prophet to voice the fact that we are now living in the perilous times that the New Testament foretells. We can observe many rebellious spirits manipulating people worldwide to act out all the negatives of selfishness listed in II Timothy and the other epistles. We must be like Timothy, who Paul charged to "stir up your spiritual gifts." We too are entrusted with the Holy Spirit's directive to bear witness to the gospel's ability to transform lives. How we live will speak louder than what we say.

Jesus prayed with expectancy that His followers would walk in the knowledge of who they are in Him, and in the same God-given authority that He has. This authority is available to each of us by the power of the Holy Spirit. We will do well to refresh ourselves often through the reading of His powerful prayer in John 17. It gives us a clear vision of our highly privileged and responsible position in Christ.

* * * * *

Prayer:

Dear Father God: You have saved me and called me with a holy calling, not according to my works or abilities, but according to Your own purpose and grace, which were given in Christ Jesus before time began. May Your dear Spirit remind and exhort me daily that I am to be illuminating light and preserving salt to my unique world. May I be engraved with the mind of Christ, for it is in His name I ask. Amen.

CHAPTER 8

Appropriate the Blood Covering

∞

Knowing that you were not redeemed with corruptible things,
like silver or gold, from your aimless conduct
received by tradition from your fathers,
but with the precious blood of Christ,
as of a lamb without blemish and without spot.
(I Peter 1:18–19)

This meditation provides us with some major reasons why believers should treasure the precious blood of Christ as a priceless spiritual endowment. It is referred to in thirteen books of the New Testament. Since blood has always been the sacrificial element in God's covenants with man, the significance of this role and importance in our right relationship with God can be more fully understood by studying the first five books of the Old Testament.

When the phrase "we plead the blood of Christ"

is included in a prayer, several vital scriptural principles are being conveyed. We want to establish what is being expressed and to also consider to whom this pronouncement would be made.

First, the blood of Jesus Christ is the establishing element of our redemption. By it we are reconciled to God the Father. It is imperative that we understand His declaration that without the shedding of blood there is no remission of sin (see Leviticus 5 and Hebrews 9:22).

It was decreed in former times that the Levitical priests were required to offer animal blood repeatedly for the people's sins as well as their own. But the Lord Jesus Christ entered the Most Holy Place with His own blood just once, and for all mankind obtained our eternal redemption (see Hebrews 7:26–27).

Secondly, we need to appropriate the precious blood as our valid identification as Christ's purchased property. The angels of God and even Satan and his followers recognize what it means whenever a believer declares he is "under the blood." This new covenant pronouncement is a holy roadblock to the enemy of our souls.

We can delight in the prophetic account in Revelation of the saints who are called "overcomers" by the blood of the Lamb and by the word of their testimony (12:11). His blood will never diminish in its effectual power for the heirs of Christ. Hallelujah!

Thirdly, we can know that the Lord's shed blood provides for our continual cleansing from the sins that we now commit. We need to quickly repent of each sin and lean heavily on the promise of I John

1:7–9 that the blood of Jesus Christ cleanses us from all confessed sin.

The fourth facet of provision relating to Christ's blood is our sanctification. Now we, more readily than the high priests of old, can boldly enter into the holy place of intimate fellowship with the Godhead: Father, Son, and Holy Spirit. The Scriptures say that we can enter in boldly now by a new and living way, which Christ consecrated for us with His blood, according to Hebrews 10:19–20. This is the "secret place" that only the Holy Spirit can introduce a believer to enjoy, on a moment-by-moment basis. No human third party needs to be involved in this spiritual fellowship between Father and child.

While these blessed provisions have been established long ago for every redeemed child of God, it enriches our souls to prayerfully acknowledge the scope of the precious blood covering of the New Testament. Exodus 12 records the Israelites obeying God's mysterious order to place the shed blood of the sacrificial lamb on their doorposts and lintels before the night of the first passover for their families' survival. We too can announce that the blood of Christ[3*] has been placed over our lives and our domains. This is a valid declaration that will strengthen our faith in God's covenant with us.

* * * * *

Prayer:
Dear Father God: I thank You for the precious blood of my Lord Jesus that was provided at such a costly price for my salvation. I consider it a most

holy element, shed for me while I was yet in my sins. It is Your identifying banner over my life. In Jesus' name I praise You. Amen.

CHAPTER 9

Appropriate the Word of God

∞

The entirety of Your word is truth,
And every one of Your righteous judgments
endures forever.
(Psalm 119:160)

It is an established fact that if a believer does not partake of the Word of God, he is without essential spiritual nourishment. The one who has come to Jesus Christ for salvation will find his newborn but undeveloped spiritual life withering away unless he draws on the Holy Scriptures to feed, direct, and sustain him.

Today's text is just one of 116 verses that David the psalmist needed in Psalm 119 to adequately proclaim his thanksgiving to God for the great treasure he found in God's written Word. And he had only part of the Old Testament! A reading of this Psalm expands our awareness of the magnitude of the

Bible's laws, commandments, principles, and promises, as well as God's historical record of His dealings with the human race.

All of mankind can be classed into only five categories in regard to partaking of God's Word. They are the uninformed, the rebellious, the slothful, those with only head knowledge, and, finally, the appropriators.

This devotional book is directed to the appropriators, those children of God who never lose their first love of following the Lord Jesus. May we all be exhorted to desire to be true, maturing disciples of Christ by continually being changed by the vital message in the Holy Bible.

Isaiah recorded this pearl of truth: "Wisdom and knowledge will be the stability of your times, and the strength of salvation; the fear of the Lord is His treasure" (33:6). This potent promise is repeated in many scriptures. As we enter the twenty-first century, we surely have need of being stable and strong. As we consistently study and act on God's truth, we are made strong for every circumstance. Whatever befalls us, we will be upheld by the sure knowledge that we are God's property and His responsibility. Although it is almost impossible to understand, He is aware and concerned about all of our situational needs at any given time.

We live in a generation that has seen a proliferation of the Bible throughout the civilized world. Because of the rapid advance of various technical means in our day, the dynamic truths of the Scriptures are available on a scale never before possible. It brings us real joy whenever we hear accounts of books of the Bible being translated into new languages.

It is a time of restoration of the whole counsel of God to His church universal. The teaching ministry has received a fresh anointing to proclaim the full gospel message. The Holy Spirit is exhorting the body of Christ to give preeminence to God's commandments and spiritual laws in every aspect of our daily lives. Those who respond will be the overcomers who are enabled to achieve spiritual maturity and fruitfulness. Jesus spoke of the special blessings for these overcomers in chapters two and three in the book of Revelation.

In later chapters, we will consider how we can enhance our spiritual journey through life as God's servants in the multi-faceted roles of His witnesses, ambassadors, praisers, watchmen, intercessors, counselors, and deliverers. All of these privileges come to those who gain a revelation of who they are in Christ from God's divine handbook, the Bible.

Believers have insufficient growth when they rely only on weekly sermons, no matter how anointed they may be. We must also feed on the Bread of Heaven individually if we desire to be the Lord's disciples. Many of the parables of Jesus emphasize this requirement. The parables of the talents, the sower, and the houses built on foundations of sand or rock all convey the importance of giving daily priority to the study of the Scriptures.

An excellent method of feeding on the Word is to memorize verses that contain commandments or promises. By meditating on these scriptural principles, we give the Holy Spirit a means of direct communication to our spirits whenever we need His specific instructions.

Let us remember that God has pronounced that His Word is alive and powerful, with a sharpness that is able to divide the soul and spirit, and is also a discerner of the thoughts and intents of our hearts (see Hebrews 4:12). This is the very means He used that brought us to a conscious need for Jesus as Savior.

After we taste and see that the Lord is good for salvation from our hopeless condition, we should go on to learn that this same creative Word gives us a new life and a reason to live in an overcoming manner. God designated Jesus Christ as the "Word of God." As we read the Bible and commune with Jesus, we will receive continual instructions, and thereby will be able to perceive God's will. This gives us abiding joy in our eternal relationship, plus a peace and hope for the future. God's ultimate purpose for preserving His Word throughout the centuries is so that Jesus Christ, the living Word, can be released in reality into sin-bound lives with a transforming power.

When we truly comprehend the perpetual anointing on the Word of God, we will follow the prompting of the Holy Spirit to step out in bold faith on its power to minister to needs. This anointing breaks the yoke of bondages: Satan's grip of sin, sickness, and death.

The book of Genesis records that God spoke all creation into being. His eternal intentions are to grant the children of God this same kind of supernatural means to change lives, and even circumstances, of those who will act and speak His words in faith. We are endowed as God's spokesmen.

* * * * *

Prayer:

Heavenly Father, today I declare that "The law of the Lord is perfect, converting the soul; the testimony of the Lord is sure, making wise the simple; the statutes of the Lord are right, rejoicing the heart; the commandment of the Lord is pure, enlightening the eyes; the fear of the Lord is clean, enduring forever; the judgments of the Lord are true and righteous altogether. More to be desired are they than gold, yea, than much fine gold; sweeter also than honey and the honeycomb. Moreover by them Your servant is warned, and in keeping them there is great reward" (Psalm 19:7–11). This is my reason for joy, I do now declare, in the name of Jesus. Amen.

CHAPTER 10

Appropriate the Keys to the Kingdom

∞

Giving thanks to the Father
who has qualified us to be partakers
of the inheritance
of the saints in the light.
He has delivered us from the power of darkness
and conveyed us into the kingdom of the Son
of His love.
(Colossians 1:12-13)

A very wise Christian stated that believers should learn to look on all of nature as a part of the kingdom of God, allowing the powers of the coming world to possess us and lift us up into life in the heavenly places. Then our hearts and our views would be enlarged to grasp a foretaste of it.[4*]

Too often we have a very limited vision of what our heavenly Father desires for us in the ages to come, as well as in this present time of preparation.

We are not meant to just settle down after our declaration of salvation as having all of our goals attained. We each have a divine destiny in Christ. This lifetime is our training ground.

We are all called by God to participate in His eternal program from the day of our salvation onward. We are disregarding our present kingdom citizenship and its responsibilities and privileges if we fail to realize that our days on earth are meant to be our training time. We restrict our present spiritual growth by thinking that we will be changed only after die and go to heaven.

While it is true that untold millennial blessings are reserved for the time beyond the second coming of Jesus to rule here on earth, many provisions are waiting for our appropriation right now. Our future kingdom assignments will be rewarded on the basis of the scriptural keys we use for spiritual growth now.

The fruit of God's Holy Spirit and the ministry gifts are primary ingredients of the Christian's present-day endowments. When we enter God's kingdom by receiving His Son as our Savior and Lord, we can either enjoy or neglect these valuable giftings.

Jesus spoke extensively on the kingdom of God during His earthly ministry. He and John the Baptist repeatedly announced, "Repent, for the kingdom of heaven is at hand" (Matthew 3:2, 4:17). The four gospels contain more than one hundred different references by Jesus to the kingdom of God. He charged His first disciples to preach on the kingdom. It is also the message of the first-century church, according to the book of Acts.

Although the glorious revealing of this visible

kingdom is still a future event, we who now believe are meant to welcome God's divine government rule into our lives now! We have the future promise of Revelation 11:15: "The kingdoms of this world have become the kingdoms of our Lord and of His Christ."

What a blessing and a rest it is to let Jesus Christ establish His throne in our hearts. He is able to govern our daily walk when we welcome His Spirit to channel our direction, our words, and our responses. This becomes possible only as we let the Word of God abide in us and learn to abide in Jesus, the living Word.

As we learn about the actual ministry responsibilities that will be part of Christ's kingdom reign, we can see many facets of these serving qualities begin to function in our lives now. Peace that flows like a river is to govern our days. His love, joy, and other positive attributes of the Spirit's fruit can be nurtured and become operative in our character, even in the midst of life's diverse and often negative situations.

We learn valuable keys of obedience that have eternal benefits as we become more sensitive to the promptings of God's Spirit. Life gives us constant opportunities for applying principles of the keys of the kingdom. We can be encouraged as we remember that Jesus said that the one who can be trusted in small matters would indeed be trusted with much weightier matters in the future (Matthew 25:23).

It is inspiring to make a study of the prophetic scriptural accounts of the actual kingdom to come. We can read that God's saints are likened to a well-trained army, highly disciplined and with much overcoming strength. It gives us a clear focus on what it means to be "partakers of the inheritance of the saints" of this chapter's Colossians theme text. This is an excellent challenge to inspire us to become overcomers through life's circumstances.

We of the present-day body of Christ can readily sense that we live in momentous yet turbulent times. No matter the length of time beforehand, there is a mounting anticipation of the nearing return of King Jesus to a most needy world. Then He will unite us with the saints of past generations for a joint participation in His glorious thousand-year reign here on earth. I want to have a part in that, don't you?

* * * * *

Prayer:

Dear heavenly Father: Again I come to You in the name of Jesus. Just as He said that He delighted to do Your will, I too desire to be able to do Your will in all things. Help me to stay sensitive to Your leading and direction in all of my relationships and circumstances. I want to grow into the person You see that I can be in Jesus. May I learn to count every trial and situation as a part of my essential grooming for Your everlasting kingdom. Amen.

CHAPTER 11

Appropriate the
Will of God

∽

*I will instruct you and teach you in the way
you should go;
I will guide you with My eye.
(Psalm 32:8)*

*For as many as are led by the Spirit of God,
these are sons of God.
(Romans 8:14)*

Undoubtedly, sincere believers desire to know
and do the will of God, yet too few feel they live
in that reality. This dilemma is addressed by today's
dual Scripture texts. In reading both the Old and
New Testaments, we soon come to realize that God's
richest blessings are liberally promised to the obedient. These blessings are part of our present-day
endowments.

From Genesis to Revelation, it is recorded that

God longs to communicate His will to His human family. The Spirit of God continually pleads throughout the Scriptures for listening ears to hear. It is exciting to live with the expectation of interacting with the living God in the midst of our personal circumstances. Just as He calls us to commune with Him through our prayers, we can also expect to be guided by Him by learning His Word or by receiving godly Scripture-based counsel.

The marvelous provision of walking in the will of God requires the key quality of patience. Our spiritual journey through life is one of mixing faith with the learning process. It is a source of great inspiration to realize that even before we became believers in Jesus Christ, God was communicating His will to us. That universal message is that we must come to the heavenly Father through Jesus, His Son.

This primary knowledge of God's will comes directly through the ministry of His Holy Spirit. We either read the gospel message ourselves, or receive it through the witness of others. This is the grace of God in action. We do not first seek Him; through His divine love, He seeks and draws us.

After our conversion experience, we find that we are then to become the seeking party for developing this eternal relationship. This is the point where some fail to actively pursue and enjoy knowing God's will. Because they are not willing to spend the dedicated time to come into an awareness of how to perceive God's will, they sacrifice the available divine leadership.

Listen to what the Father and the Son say to every believer: "Then you will call upon Me and go and pray to Me, and I will listen to you. And you will seek Me and find Me, when you search for Me with all your heart" (Jeremiah 29:12–13).

This is the familiar challenging promise of Jesus: "If you abide in My word, you are My disciples indeed. And you shall know the truth, and the truth shall make you free" (John 8:31–32). Those who walk in the truth can also walk in God's will. No one can specifically tell us how to daily appropriate the will of God other than to point out that His will is to be found in His Word. As we consistently saturate our mind with Scripture, we will be filled with that knowledge.

We must "eat the Word" until it becomes a vital part of our responses in our spirits, souls, and bodies. When we digest the Bible's truth, it can then be the deciding and controlling factor in our reactions to circumstances and people. An excellent place to meditate on this principle is John 6:25–63. Here Jesus refers to Himself as "the bread from heaven." He assured His followers that whoever eats of this bread will live forever. Although it is sometimes assumed that He was speaking of only His ordinance of the communion, can we consider that He also distinctly implied spiritually consuming and digesting the written Word? It seems we can, based on the fact that the gospel of John begins by stating, "In the beginning was the Word, and the Word was *with* God, and the Word *was* God."

In seeking to know the will of God, we are expected only to act on what we now know. A step at a time, His Spirit is able to unfold what we are to do. We can be guided by peace. When there is an uncertain lack of peace, it is always wise to precede action with prayer. Our part is to walk in the revealed will of God as we know it. For example, a parent does not need to seek God's further will in the matter of caring for his family's needs. A businessperson does not have to tarry to decide that it is right to show up at his place of employment. These are all settled matters in the specific principles in the Word of God for taking care of known and present responsibilities.

At times we hear of God opening or closing doors of expected opportunity. This can be observed as an individual looks back on his own past. Often he is either allowed to enter a new venture or is kept from harm's way by invisible guidance. This can be a mix of knowledge and/or the providence of God—grace and works combined. Sometimes a person will have an immediate awareness of the direction or the protection of the Holy Spirit through His conviction impacting the mind.

The counsel of other mature and committed Christians is a sound avenue for confirmation when one may be uncertain in determining an important decision. This is one of the ministries of our pastors and elders. Real spiritual perception comes to the soul quickly in understanding the fear of the Lord.

As Christians, we can live in this blessing only as we renew our minds and become like-minded to Christ. The recent expression, "What would Jesus do?" is a good reality check when we are in doubt. We must take quality time to receive the various subtle leadings available to us for our choices in life's matters. This is the essence of our dual theme texts.

It is the dedicated commitment of applying the Lord's commandments to our ordinary daily lives in ways that can be at times extraordinary.

* * * * *

Prayer:

Dear Father God: My desire is to walk in Your will that I may be pleasing in Your sight and usable in Your service. The Lord *is* my Shepherd; I shall not want. He does lead, provide, and protect me. He restores my soul and leads me in the paths of righteousness for His Name's sake. I seek Your Spirit of wisdom and revelation in the knowledge of Jesus my Lord. Amen.

CHAPTER 12

Appropriate the Mind of Christ

∞

Now we have received, not the spirit of the world,
but the Spirit who is from God,
that we might know the things that have been freely
given to us by God.
For "who has known the mind of the Lord that he
may instruct Him?"
But we have the mind of Christ.
(I Corinthians 2:12, 16)

Each day our lives are made up of a series of choices and decisions. Whether we are students, homemakers, or company CEOs, we all must choose among many options that come along. Some choices are minor and can be made quickly; others can be life changing and take real consideration.

Battles are won or lost by human judgments. In business, profit or loss is the result of somebody's decisions. Even relationships can be established or broken by a single determination. As we all look back at our personal choices, we sometimes agonize over what might have been. How often we wish we could "buy back" bad judgments! Great stress is often experienced through an inability to make up our minds. We long for someone else's wisdom to make those important decisions.

For the believer in Jesus Christ, a tremendous privilege is presented in the verses of our theme text. It is interesting to note that in the Greek Diaglot, verse 16 is rendered, "We possess the mind of Christ." What a fantastic statement: to have or possess the mind of Christ. Yet so few comprehend this awesome potential, or strive to attain it: to have the availability of Christ's mind in making our daily decisions. This is what leads to living the abundant life that Jesus spoke about.

Too many Christians settle for the opposite. We often fail to consider what the Lord thinks about a matter. We remember the often-quoted verse of Isaiah 55:8: "'For My thoughts are not your thoughts, nor are your ways My ways,' says the Lord." This Old Testament statement could short-circuit our attempt to let God enter into our daily decision-making. But we now have the indwelling ministry of God's Spirit to help us make wise choices.

By reading the entire fifty-fifth chapter of Isaiah, we understand that God is speaking here to the unrighteous man—it is a plea to the unregenerate person to come to God and hear of His ways. Whenever anyone responds to God's call, he has the opportunity to exchange his worldly ways and thoughts for that of God's divine ways. Once we come into a right relationship to God the Father, by receiving Jesus Christ as Lord, God does not benefit by having His children remain ignorant of His ways. His desire, expressed in both the Old and New Testaments, is that we begin to think as He does and act accordingly. This is having the mind of Christ, and it can come about only as we seek the wisdom of God in the Bible.

A vast panorama of possibilities presents itself through the concept of tapping into the mind of Christ. First of all, we will be pleasing to our heavenly Father and Jesus our Lord. By desiring to live with the mind of Christ in control, our words, deeds, and even our thoughts can be brought under the wisdom of His Holy Spirit. We can also be usable to His purposes as we allow His scriptural principles to govern our decisions and actions.

It is true that we won't be without error in our daily choices or be entirely free from human frailty in our manner of conduct. But as we daily study the Scriptures, and then meditate on the commandments and biblical principles, the positive changes will come.

No generation of believers has yet fully walked in this dimension of spiritual dynamics. Yet the keys or steps have been clearly laid out and are available to the most elementary Bible student. We currently have a Christian phrase circulating: "What would Jesus do?" When the mind of Christ is applied to our choices, we are partaking of the divine source of wisdom.

The Bible contains the spiritual laws and principles that God has established for our good. The New Testament is God's covenant or contract with us. It presents us with all the rules for righteous living. Through obedience to God's Word, we establish our decisions on the royal laws of His kingdom. It activates the blessings of our Father for a fruitful, abundant life.

Even in pressing circumstances, those who come into the knowledge of this open secret are able to walk victoriously on the highway of the upright, as pictured in Proverbs 16:17. This book is still a pattern for successful living in all of our relationships. Proverbs begins with a clear expression of God's call to a people who will seek His knowledge and instruction. Then He adds the promise of divine assistance: "Surely I will pour out my spirit on you; I will make my words known to you" (1:23).

Why do so few know the liberty that applying the mind of Christ can bring? Even earnest Bible students and scholars in each generation have, for the most part, lived far below their potential. Though we read God's Word and even have a love of it, too often we stop at this point. We readily agree it is good, yet we promptly turn our attention to the occupation of the day, neglecting to apply the wisdom we have fed on. We fail to comprehend that we are to consistently apply biblical commandments and principles to every circumstance.

These God-breathed directives were designed to bring us into line with the mind of Christ, both at home and in the market place. In the simplest of understanding, it is being able to determine what scriptural response Jesus would apply to our choices and decisions. I John 2:6 states: "He who says he abides in Him ought himself also to walk just as He walked." This will come about only as we continue in personal Bible study times and as we prayerfully seek to know the promptings of God's Holy Spirit within for guidance. This means taking the Word of God in and digesting it to the point that it can and will be expressed through our thoughts and actions.

Jesus explained this in John 8:31–32: "If you abide in My word, you are My disciples indeed. And you shall know the truth, and the truth shall make you free." It is more profitable to read this complete section of His teaching in John 15. Making the decision to follow this discipleship role is second only to deciding to receive Jesus as Savior and Lord. It is the true essence of the Christian experience. There is no real life for the believer apart from the Word of God. In John 15, Jesus said that we would either be a fruitful branch or dead wood!

The exhortation and rich promise of Romans 12:2 says, "And do not be conformed to this world, but be transformed by the renewing of your mind, that you may prove what is that good and acceptable and perfect will of God."

* * * * *

Prayer:

Dear heavenly Father: How I realize that I need the mind and wisdom of Christ every day of my life. In Jesus' name, I ask You to renew and deepen my hunger for Your Word and Your Holy Spirit's ministry. I realize that I must increase my knowledge of Your commandments and principles by meditating and memorizing Scripture promises. Amen.

CHAPTER 13

Appropriate the Armor of God

∽

Finally, my brethren, be strong in the Lord
and in the power of His might.
Put on the whole armor of God, that you
may be able to stand against the wiles
of the devil.
(Ephesians 6:10–11)

For some believers in Jesus Christ, it comes as a distinct surprise that we have any need for armor in the Christian life. The Apostle Paul, who was often on the front lines of spiritual battles, is stating here, under divine inspiration, that having protective spiritual gear is essential.

Throughout the Bible, numerous references are made both to armies and their equipment. God conscripted His first army in the Sinai wilderness (Numbers 1:2–3). He commanded the people, through Moses, to number the men of each tribe, and then ordered them to destroy their enemies to gain the land of promise.

Under our New Testament covenant, God's program is still in force. All believers are appointed their places in the Lord's army. Protective armor is available to us, but its effect is more complete when we are aware of and appropriate this spiritual covering. Every soldier when giving his equipment is required to inspect it and to learn how each piece operates. We also need to acutely examine the "armor of God" and the suitable mindset that is listed in Ephesians 6. Once we understand that the Christian is to do overcoming battle with the forces of spiritual evil, we will, with much appreciation, don each piece as permanent apparel.

Let us carefully consider each part of our equipment, as well as the Holy Spirit's challenge through Paul to "take up the whole armor of God, that you may be able to withstand in the evil day, and having done all, to stand. Stand therefore, having girded your waist with *truth,* having put on the *breastplate of righteousness,* and having shod your feet with the *preparation of the gospel of peace;* above all, taking the *shield of faith* with which you will be able to quench all the fiery darts of the wicked one. And take the *helmet of salvation,* and the *sword of the Spirit,* which is the word of God; *praying* always with all prayer and supplication in the Spirit, being watchful to this end with all perseverance and supplication for all the saints" (Ephesians 6:13–18, emphasis added).

This essential equipment for believers includes all seven of the above emphasized components: a belt of truth, the breastplate of righteousness, the knowledge of the gospel of peace, the shield of faith, the helmet of salvation, the Word of God, and a persevering prayer life. It is important to realize that just as a soldier does not provide his own uniform and equipment, we Christians have already been issued everything we will need to be spiritually equipped to serve our heavenly Commander. We further need to be aware that we have a commandment to actively accept these available provisions; they are seldom activated automatically.

The uninformed believer often falls prey to satanic attacks and many negative persuasions. Since they are unaware of who is causing their woes, they feel both defeated and guilty. Paul describes our enemies very distinctly in verse 12: "For we do not wrestle against flesh and blood, but against principalities, against powers, against the rulers of the darkness of this age, against spiritual hosts of wickedness in the heavenly places."

Though these unseen enemies of God are valid threats, we are not to live in fear or dread. We are told that with the use of our armor, we can gain the upper hand in any spiritual encounter. Our victorious position is also confirmed in II Corinthians 10:4: "For the weapons of our warfare are not carnal but mighty in God for pulling down strongholds."

Once again, we return to the basic fact that we must know what the Bible says to live the triumphant Christian life! Jesus has given us His authority to stand against and call a halt to every illegal act of satanic wickedness. The four gospels make us aware that Jesus was operating from the position of righteousness with the same equipment we are now analyzing. He is our example for the mode of operation against evil. The New Testament epistles give us the knowledge of and the precise directions for using each of these seven components of our armor.

Our defensive or offensive stance in using the Word of God as the sword of the Spirit must be vocalized. We can begin to practice feeling comfortable by declaring aloud, in the mighty name of Jesus, that we and our homes are covered by His precious blood. We can confess the truth that our families and our abodes are now God's property and even that all who enter will walk in peace.

When we speak forth the truth of Scripture, several valuable elements occur. We hear and gain strength and assurance as we claim what is already rightfully ours. The Lord also hears and is blessed by our new birthright declaration. If any spiritual enemies are around, they too will hear and recognize that we are taking dominion. Scripture states they have to flee!

Speaking aloud in this manner has much power, just as our spoken prayers have a definite value. This will give us the boldness to speak out in personal ministry to others as they relate to us that they are under duress and are open to our help.

When Jesus returns to earth with His kingdom rule, Revelation 19:14 tells of armies accompanying Him. Today He is continuing to recruit soldiers who will allow themselves to be discipled by the Holy Spirit. We are to be in His service now and in the ages yet to come. We can agree with the charge found in I Thessalonians 5:8: "But let us who are of the day be sober, putting on the breastplate of faith and love, and as a helmet the hope of salvation."

We will gain motivation to become a part of this purely voluntary royal army by taking note of the rewards assigned to the "overcomers" of Revelation 2 and 3. One might feel that these promises of reward are only for the future, but this is not so, for as each promise is stated, it is also specified, "He who has an ear, let him hear what the Spirit says to the churches." This is the church age; we need to be overcomers now!

The present-day members of the global church of Jesus Christ are now in training to overcome. We are to overcome self, sin, and Satan. We are learning to reign during this lifetime with Jesus Christ as Lord so we will be prepared to reign with Him in the age to come.

* * * * *

Prayer:

Dear heavenly Father: In the name of Jesus, I want to be a part of that company of people who are strong in the power of the Lord. I do now don the armor that You have supplied for me. I firmly secure the belt of Your truth; I gladly put on the breastplate of righteousness. I am thankful that I will walk in peace through the preparation of the gospel. With joy I take up the shield of faith, which gives me authority to quench all the fiery, accusing darts of the wicked one. Salvation is my sure helmet; I know I am Yours. Your Word is my anointed sword, but I will not harm my brethren. My prayers from this day forth will be in the name of my Lord and King, Jesus Christ, who paid the ultimate price for my spiritual apparel, and gave me the privilege to serve. Amen.

CHAPTER 14

Appropriate Your Angelic Support

∞

The angel of the Lord encamps all around those
who fear Him, and delivers them.
(Psalm 34:7)

And of the angels He says:
"Who makes His angels spirits And His ministers a
flame of fire."
Are they not all ministering spirits sent forth
to minister for those who will inherit salvation?
(Hebrews 1:7, 14)

The angels of God throughout Scripture are present in the affairs of mankind. These mysterious
and awesome beings that God created in some dis-
tant eon of time are still spoken of in the New
Testament era. Although artists consistently give
them soft and feminine features, if visible, we would
no doubt be astounded at their stately and herculean

attributes.

God's prophet Elisha was greatly strengthened when he realized that his battle with the Syrians was supernaturally reinforced by a mighty invisible army of angelic beings. He prayed that God would allow his faltering servant also to see them, and then he likewise was strengthened (II Kings 6:17).

The Bible records that God's people often knew with a certainty that they had been ministered to by angels. At times they were indiscernible to the human eye; on other occasions they appeared in human form and even in contemporary apparel. The Bible records in a matter-of-fact way their feats of supernatural strength in resolving the impossible predicaments of the saints. As you read today's texts, didn't you find you were being greatly encouraged to realize that you have the personal attendance and concern of heaven's mighty angels? How often the remembrance of their silent vigil has stilled a believer's fear. Although much mystery cloaks the role of angels, we must rely on the significant factual information God has supplied to those who penned both the Old and New Testaments.

Let us consider what angelic support we can appropriate today, based wholly on God's revelation. In Psalm 91, we have this assurance: "Because you have made the Lord, who is my refuge, even the Most High, your dwelling place, no evil shall befall you, nor shall any plague come near your dwelling; for He shall give His angels charge over you, to keep you in all your ways. In their hands they shall bear you up, lest you dash your foot against a stone" (verses 9–12). This promise is repeated in Matthew

4:6 and Luke 4:10–11. Here Satan is speaking to Jesus, saying that even he knows there is angelic protection for God's children.

Note that the requirement in the above Psalm is for believers to make the Lord their habitation. This is dwelling or abiding in Christ, making our position "in Him" our permanent yet mobile abode. We become established in the realization that no matter where we go, as believers we have the Holy Spirit of Christ in residence.

It is a logical deduction that being "in Christ" is to be residing in the secret place of the Most High of Psalm 91. We are declared to be abiding under the shadow of the Almighty when we have the confession that we trust Him as our refuge and fortress (verses 1, 2). The term "in Christ" is used often in the New Testament.

References to angels give us the distinct understanding that they are definitely not to be exalted above Jesus or ever worshipped in any manner. They are ministering spirits that the Lord sends forth to minister to those who will inherit salvation.

Angels announced the birth of Jesus and continued to attend Him during all of His earthly life. The book of Acts relates that the disciples had the ministry of angels in directing their paths, releasing their chains, and opening prison doors. The scoffer may say that this documented supernatural assistance of angels was strictly to help get the first-century church started. But as we still hear reports of angelic activity today, with some doubting, we still must consider why Hebrews 13:2 warns us not to forget to entertain strangers, as we may be unknowingly *"entertaining angels."*

We do not want to be presumptuous with any of the gracious promises of God, but we can lay claim to any of the biblical provisions when we meet the stated qualifications. For instance, we can't be idlers and expect angels to perform our responsibilities, but just realizing angels are invisibly supporting us gives great motivation to carry out our required actions. Jesus gave believers alone the commission to convey the gospel message; this is not the assignment of His angelic host. However, He did say that when a sinner repents after receiving the gospel witness, angels share in heaven's joy.

On the basis of these several Scriptures, we can with prayer and thanksgiving request the attending ministry of angels, or in our intercession for others. The frequent testimony of believers who live alone is that they find much comfort and peace in an awareness of angels. They can petition Father God, directly from His Word, that His holy angels will stand guard during the long night hours. Parents can rest better by thanking God that the protective promises of Jesus are still true. Matthew 18:10 states: "Take heed that you do not despise one of these little ones, for I say to you that in heaven their angels always see the face of My Father who is in heaven." Our children have designated angels. We can request in our prayers that they be "on duty" when we can't.

These timeless angels of God ministered effectively in the past; they still minister during this church age, and they will be fulfilling their specific assignments in the future. We have the promises of a glorious day when the world will see Jesus Christ, revealed from heaven, and His mighty angels will be with Him visibly. In the heavenly Jerusalem to follow, the city of the living God, there will be a company of innumerable angels. Shouldn't we consider and appreciate them in their present reality?

* * * * *

Prayer:

Dear Father God: You have written much about angels. I do not want to ever place undue emphasis on their role in Your purposes. Jesus Christ is Lord of all. Help me as I study the Scriptures to understand and enjoy the proper role You have allotted angels in this present time. In Jesus' name I ask, Amen.

CHAPTER 15

Appropriate Your Spiritual Authority

∽

*All authority has been given to Me in heaven
and on earth.
Go therefore and make disciples of all the nations,
baptizing them in the name of the Father and of the
Son and of the Holy Spirit,
teaching them to observe all things that I
have commanded you;
and lo, I am with you always,
even to the end of the age.
(Matthew 28:18–20)*

The deepest yearning of the Father's heart is that all of His children will act on these clear instructions issued by Jesus to those first-century disciples and all who will follow Him. We are still to be ministers of His new covenant in the midst of our everyday activities.

God's purpose is to have a people like Himself, a

family of believers who are of one mind and one spirit with Him. A wise teacher stated it well, that the Father's deepest longing is that so much of Himself be manifested through all believers that the things of this world would bow down before the light of God that is in us.

It is an astounding fact that God places His faith in us! His regenerated children are His chosen messengers for proclaiming the gospel message that Jesus Christ is the Savior of the world. When we read in Acts 1:8 that Jesus declared to His followers that they were to be His witnesses, we know they believed Him, for they soon prayed for holy boldness to do so (4:29–33). They even had faith to ask for signs and wonders. The record shows that their prayers were answered. It is stated that multitudes believed. Should we be expecting any less today when needy souls are so greatly multiplied? The state of the world today has caused many to be in the harvest fields of decision.

Although we walk in newness of life as believers in Jesus, we are a minority. The secular world often ridicules Christians and scoffs at things of the Spirit that they cannot perceive or understand. They say, "seeing is believing." Our salvation experience turns this proverb around; now believing is seeing as our spiritual vision begins to function. What a privilege to appropriate the spiritual authority that is so essential to living the victorious Christian life. We are known of God and are chosen to be endowed with His Spirit to minister in the authority of Jesus' name.

In each of these chapters, we are reviewing the endowments that God desires to invest in our lives that will produce deliverance, healing, and salvation for those whose lives we touch. We are to serve apprenticeships that will form us into the image of the pattern Son, Jesus Christ. He said, "He who believes in Me, the works that I do he will do also; and greater works than these he will do, because I go to My Father" (John 14:12). These are the results He expects through believers who will follow in His steps.

Upon first learning that we have been given authority, we may sense timidity that it is not for everyone. But God has not given us the spirit of fear, but of power, love, and a sound mind. Our assurance will grow in proportion to the way we digest scriptural truth. Just as an apprentice follows his teacher's instructions, so the sincere Christian is to be obedient to his teacher, the Holy Spirit. We will grow into the authority that is taught in the Scriptures. Isaiah's promise is still valid, which declares: "'No weapon formed against you shall prosper, and every tongue which rises against you in judgment you shall condemn. This is the heritage of the servants of the Lord, and their righteousness is from Me,' says the Lord" (Isaiah 54:17).

Since believers are called "servants of righteousness" in both the Old and New Testaments, what does this entail? In Luke 4:18–19, we have a rich condensation: "The Spirit of the Lord is upon Me, because He has anointed Me to preach the gospel to the poor; He has sent Me to heal the brokenhearted, to proclaim liberty to the captives and recovery of sight to the blind, to set at liberty those who are oppressed; to proclaim the acceptable year of the

Lord." This outline of the ministry of Jesus should also be the essence of the Christian's life today. We are to also take authority over sin, sickness, demons, and fear.

Jesus said, "Blessed are those who hunger and thirst for righteousness, for they shall be filled" (Matthew 5:6). Before we can take authority over the bonds or blindness of another, we must first use our God-given authority to loose ourselves from all sin and the bondage of fear. We can then walk in the newness of life at the prompting of the Holy Spirit. As we put away the hindrances we are made aware of, we are also motivated to see others set free. The means to realize this and all of the blessings Jesus spoke about is by regularly "feeding" on the Word of God. Our spiritual liberty and authority should be an expression of our daily lives. As we have our minds renewed by divine knowledge, we will become salt and light to others. As we present the light of the gospel, they will become thirsty to learn for themselves.

Today we see a measure of the salt and light in evidence throughout the world. But in view of the many millions who declare they are Christ's, His reflected light should be dazzling the world. It will happen only when each member of His body truly responds to his "servant of righteousness" role through appropriating his spiritual authority.

* * * * *

Prayer:
Dear Father God: We thank You that You trust us

with a rich heritage as Your servants of righteousness. Help me realize that the source of my ministry to those who need the life of Jesus Christ is in Him and in the power of His name. In the name of Jesus, I pray for the same holy boldness of Your first disciples to follow the inner voice of Your Holy Spirit day by day. Amen.

CHAPTER 16

Appropriate Your Witness Role

∞

But you are a chosen generation,
a royal priesthood,
a holy nation, His own special people,
that you may proclaim the praises of Him who
called you out of darkness into
His marvelous light.
(I Peter 2:9)

The New Testament is liberally saturated with God's mandate that every believer is to be a witness to the reality of His Son, Jesus Christ, being the Savior of the world. This is both our high privilege and our responsibility. The argument is at times presented that due to natural timidity or lack of biblical knowledge, some people are excused from their roles as witnesses. But the fact is that once they declare that they are Christians, their lives become witnesses.

The world has always observed and made comment on the actions and conduct of professing Christians. Whatever we say or do, whether positive or negative, we are testifying to the quality of our believing faith. Once we recognize this, it should temper and change some of our responses and reactions. What serves to take the pressure off appropriating our witness role is to realize that a witness can tell only what he or she has seen or knows by personal experience. Believers are required only to give an account of the present knowledge they have of the Godhead and divine things. When one has nothing to tell, it would seem to be a most fragile relationship at best.

As we read of the normal witnessing lives of the first-century believers, we have the primary examples of what Jesus set in motion when He declared, "But you shall receive power when the Holy Spirit has come upon you; and you shall be witnesses to Me in Jerusalem, and in all Judea and Samaria, and to the end of the earth" (Acts 1:8).

He never intended that just a certain select group of each generation of His followers was to be designated "witnesses" and that was to be their unique life work. God's sovereign plan is that when Jesus Christ is invited into each individual life, His life and characteristics would begin flowing out of the believer's life and would produce a vital witness.

Many believers attest to the fact that while they began as almost "silent service" Christians, they eventually came to a time of vocalizing their faith. Scriptures were presented to them to reveal that while they had received Jesus as Savior, they must also go on to desire that their lives be totally placed under His control. They made Jesus both Savior and Lord!

When Thomas the disciple really understood the painful, sacrificial death of Jesus on the cross, then he was able to proclaim, "My Lord and my God!" (John 20:28). We have the full assurance that when we announce that we are yielding and even welcoming Jesus' lordship over our lives, He is very aware of it, according to I Corinthians 12:3b. The Christian who enjoys a natural witness life by yielding to the lordship of Christ and allowing God's Spirit to take a rightful position in his life will have both the desire and the ability to attest to the realty of divine truth.

Jesus was anointed for service at a specific point in His earthly life. At that time, He read the blueprint of His earthly ministry from Isaiah 61, which is recorded in Luke 4:18–19. This is what the Holy Spirit is now fully able to develop in each of our lives as we ask for His infilling or baptism. In chapter three, we covered this empowering for service. Although the Holy Spirit is resident in us from the time of our conversion, we must actively appropriate or partake of all the spiritual endowments that the Spirit of God is so willing to provide.

The New English Bible translation of Luke 11:13 gives this spiritual principle an added clarification: "If you, then, bad as you are, know how to give your children what is good for them, how much more will the heavenly Father give the Holy Spirit to those who ask Him."

When we daily seek the leading of God's Spirit, it may come so naturally that we can almost fail to recognize it. At times it is merely an impression to do a simple act, such as making a cheerful phone call, writing a letter, or assisting a stranger in the marketplace. Most of us will never be in the pulpit or in the limelight. We will have our best opportunities to witness the love of Christ to those we will encounter on a one-to-one basis.

Each of us has a unique circle of influence. For some it in is the workplace, where our best and worst sides eventually surface. We also have witness opportunities in social settings. But foremost, we live our Christian witness in our homes, among loved ones and guests. All we need to remember is that when we responded to the call of Jesus through the witness of others, we became "His workmanship, created in Christ Jesus for good works, which God prepared beforehand that we should walk in them," according to Ephesians 2:10.

* * * * *

Prayer:
Dear heavenly Father: I come to You in Jesus' name, declaring that I desire to be the called, the chosen, and the faithful witness to Your great love. It is my joy to proclaim the praises of Your Son's salvation and mercy to those You put in my path. Amen.

CHAPTER 17

Appropriate Your Serving Role

∞

And whatever you do, do it heartily,
as to the Lord and not to men,
knowing that from the Lord you will receive
the reward of the inheritance;
for you serve the Lord Christ.
(Colossians 3:23–24)

Living as we do in an ego-pleasing society, it is thought unusual to emulate the voluntary serving role. Today's secular best-selling book list is about how to look out for number one—becoming master of the game, or getting one's personal needs filled and ambitions met. Jesus taught just the opposite. He repeatedly told His disciples that the serving role was the path to blessings and fulfillment. Our heavenly Father delights to find a child of His who is an expression of His merciful compassion.

It has been stated that our salvation does not

preempt our responsibilities. The only way we can be the "light" and "salt" that Jesus spoke about is by serving others by meeting their needs. The surest way of witnessing to the calling of God on our lives is in ministering to others with our attention, our resources, or—most importantly—our time. While worldly pride is repelled by the idea of servanthood, believers who heed the leading of the Holy Spirit are enjoying secret blessings from the Lord.

You recall that Jesus said that His "meat" was to do the will of the Father. In like manner, the servants of the Lord have always testified that they receive from His supply when they have been willing to serve. At times they receive tangible things for their physical needs, and other times they receive intangible blessings for the soul and the spirit because they have obeyed the Spirit's prompting to serve in some manner.

When we come to realize that the highest calling is to be the bondservant of the Lord, it can take the sting out of giving up our most precious possession—our time. Even more than guarding our assets, we find that forfeiting a block of time away from our own pursuits is often done with much calculation. Whether our intended schedule is for work or play, the human ego is reluctant to meet another's needs before its own.

How did the writers of the New Testament, who often addressed themselves as "servants of the Lord," come to terms with the paradox that through Jesus Christ they were servants, and yet royal sons of God? Their secret was that they allowed the Holy Spirit to instruct them in the truth that to be earnest followers of Jesus would mean also living crucified lives. When the Apostle Paul penned the letter to the Philippians, he painted a graphic word picture of the humbled and exalted Christ. The crucifixion is the zenith of servanthood! By prayerfully reading this portion of Scripture, we can come to an enlightened awareness of what our priorities should be.

The vicarious death of Jesus on Calvary's cross gives us our justification and mandate to live as God's bondservants. When He yielded His will into the Father's hands, it cost Him His life. When we place our lives and our wills into the Father's hands, Jesus promised us "the abundant life." This is a life supplied by His virtue flowing through our service.

What do those first-century apostles say to encourage each of us to embrace the serving role? Paul said, "For to me, to live is Christ" (Philippians 1:21). James stated, "But he who looks into the perfect law of liberty and continues in it, and is not a forgetful hearer but a doer of the work, this one will be blessed in what he does" (James 1:25). Peter implored, "And above all things have fervent love for one another. . . . As each one has received a gift, minister it to one another, as good stewards of the manifold grace of God" (I Peter 4:8, 10). John testified, "He who says he abides in Him ought himself also to walk just as He walked" (I John 2:6).

Mastering the serving role that best authenticates the Christian life is a lifetime assignment. When our zeal for the new life in Christ wanes, or we become weary at any time, we can re-ignite both our ardor and our strength by remembering that being available to Father God is our first priority and should become our highest goal and desire. Although His gifts and callings to serve are many and varied, when we fit into our places in the body of Christ, we complement and further the present-day purposes of God. It is by continually being nurtured and fortified in the Scriptures that we will mature into the beloved, unique, and useful children of God.

* * * * *

Prayer:

Dear heavenly Father: Forgive me when I put my interests and endeavors above the quiet directions of Your Spirit. I want to make it my testimony that I must be about My Father's business. Grant me, in the blessed name of Jesus, the grace to be Your bondservant in this needy world at my doorstep. Amen.

CHAPTER 18

Appropriate the Life of Praise

∞

It is good to give thanks to the Lord,
and to sing praises to Your name, O Most High;
to declare Your lovingkindness in the morning,
and Your faithfulness every night.
(Psalm 92:1–2)

Believers who learn to be praisers are nourished by an inner joy that circumstances cannot block out. Bad news or adverse circumstances can cause real pain and grief, but when we have become people of praise, we are fortified with an unshakable foundation. It imprints our souls and spirits when we glorify God, both for who He is and what He has done.

Our heavenly Father is blessed by the praises of His children. Isaiah penned that God said, "This people I have formed for Myself; they shall declare My praise" (Isaiah 43:21). Although over twenty-five hundred years have passed, the vocal tributes of the redeemed are still a sweet essence to the Godhead.

If we were to make a list of all the reasons to continually offer praises to our God, we would find it had no ending. His bountiful mercies are beyond our ability to number them. Whenever we open the Bible, we come across many reasons to give our heavenly Father lavish thanksgiving. In addition to being continually grateful for our salvation and the assurance of a magnificent eternal destiny, we praise Him because He hears our feeblest prayer and leads and comforts us with His presence and His Word.

It is always overwhelming to consider that the God of the whole universe has such love for His children. Like Mary, we can readily cry out, "My soul magnifies the Lord, and my spirit has rejoiced in God my Savior. For He who is mighty has done great things for me, and holy is His name" (Luke 1:46, 47, 49). Maybe you say we can't use Mary's prayer. She was praising God because His Holy Spirit had overshadowed her for the conception of His Son Jesus. But hasn't the Holy Spirit of God overshadowed each of us also so that the Spirit of Christ would be born in us?

The art of praise is a learned ability. Just as our vocabulary started with one word, we also progress from that point in first appropriating and then enjoying a life of praise. Just thinking about all that we have received from our heavenly Father triggers a flow of adoration. The Apostle Peter attested that believers are "a chosen generation, a royal priesthood, a holy nation, His own special people, that you may proclaim the praises of Him who called you out of darkness into His marvelous light" (I Peter 2:9).

The forms that our praises take are also highly varied. We can quietly praise the Lord on our beds without disturbing another's rest, or we can make a happy noise and sing our glad praises. The corporate vocal praise of a congregation of believers multiplies our joy. It also puts any demonic activity on the run. Satan's crowd hates true worship. Believers testify that even when alone and sensing the dark forces of harassment, their vigorous songs of praise and clapping has dispelled the annoying torments of Satan's minions.

One of the numerous blessings of returning often to the book of Psalms is that it gives us many avenues of praise to follow. We learn that the King of Glory has robed us in His garments of righteousness. He is a covenant-keeping sovereign who abides in the midst of His people. The atoning blood of Jesus our Savior has been delivered to the very throne of God the Father on our behalf. We have been made a part of the family of God. We can rejoice exceedingly because He is aware of our circumstances. Our God is the miracle-working Creator.

How thankful we can be that Jesus, the High Priest of the New Covenant, has provided a way for us to come into the presence of a holy God, and that this compassionate High Priest will intercede on our behalf. Our daily praise should also give recognition to the indwelling Holy Spirit, who releases us from fear, want, and loneliness. We can readily extol the power of God's written Word that it not only frees us from ignorance, but also gives us directions to the abundant life in Christ.

The life of praise leads us into a life of true worship. Whereas in praising we may be speaking of what we have received from God, true worship is centering in on the supreme majesty and the glory of who He is!

* * * * *

Prayer:
Dear gracious Father: Cause Your people to increase our capacity to appropriate the noble life of praise. You are indeed the King of Kings and the Lord of Lords. You have lifted us out of darkness into the light of Your eternal kingdom. May our mouths be ever filled with our praises. It is in Jesus' name I ask this. Amen.

CHAPTER 19

Appropriate Your Ambassadorship

∞

Now all things are of God, who has reconciled us
to Himself through Jesus Christ,
and has given us the ministry of reconciliation.
Now then, we are ambassadors for Christ,
as though God were pleading through us:
we implore you on Christ's behalf,
be reconciled to God.
(II Corinthians 5:18, 20)

Isn't it treasured knowledge that our God has designated all of His children as His ambassadors? He has deposited great trust into our care. We know we are to have faith in Him; here we read that He has placed His faith in us.

An ambassador is defined as a diplomatic official of the highest rank, sent by a sovereign or a state as an authorized representative. That person is entitled and trustworthy to speak for the one who appoints him. When we read and consider today's theme text, it should have a triple effect. We should hold in high regard the fact that our heavenly Father places us in such a responsible position. We have been chosen and called to be spokesmen for the God of the universe. It is not a presumptuous thought to realize that we are persons of value.

The second effect of coming to understand that we are called ambassadors is that it should make us most anxious to learn what we are authorized to say to the world around us. It is only by reading God's Word that we gain that knowledge. Nothing is more barren in terms of communication than an uninformed spokesman. We are often dealing with life or death issues in the spirit realm. We are ambassadors called to offer people eternal life through receiving Jesus Christ. Even the newest believer who faithfully starts reading the Scriptures will have the prompting of God's Spirit when a witness opportunity happens. We can rely on the drawing power of the Holy Spirit working in others' hearts to cause them to open to what we share. Maybe it will be the portion of the Bible we have just read today.

Sometimes it is through the ministry of many witnesses that an unsaved person is brought to the point of conviction in realizing his need of the Savior and the new birth experience. We come to understand that we need not be anxious for immediate results of our ministry—we just share our faith with others, and then God will continue wooing them.

We can be encouraged by many statements in II Corinthians regarding ministry. Listen to what is recorded in chapter four: "Therefore, since we have this ministry, as we have received mercy, we do not lose heart. But we have renounced the hidden things of shame, not walking in craftiness nor handling the word of God deceitfully, but by manifestation of the truth commending ourselves to every man's conscience in the sight of God" (vv. 1–2).

The third effect of appropriating our ambassadorship is a new consciousness of what comes out of our mouths. We must come to realize that we no longer speak for ourselves alone. Our words carry power, either positive or negative. We can bless or we can curse through our spoken words. The old wartime slogan said, "Loose lips sink ships." It was to remind people in the World War II era that carelessly given information could have very grave consequences.

Take notice of the many scriptural exhortations and warnings in regard to watching our words. Ephesians has this caution for those who have "learned Christ" in having both heard and been taught by Him: "Therefore, putting away lying, 'Let each one of you speak truth with his neighbor,' for we are members of one another" (4:25). The New Testament states that we have the privilege of speaking words that are wise, gentle, gracious, fitting life-giving, and acceptable to God. Negative talk is called unprofitable, vain, idle, foolish, seditious, deceitful, and evil.

Jesus had much to teach His disciple-ambassadors about their regard for choosing words carefully. "A good man out of the good treasure of his heart brings forth good things, and an evil man out of the evil treasure brings forth evil things. But I say to you that for every idle word men may speak, they will give account of it in the day of judgment. For by your words you will be justified, and by your words you will be condemned" (Matthew 12:35–37). A friend said that when he and his wife learned this passage, their conversations were almost cut in half. They understood the seriousness of this principle of conduct.

We have stayed long on the importance of our words in today's theme of being God's ambassadors because they are our primary tools. We must become acutely aware that if we serve effectively, it is not because of any physical abilities or mental prowess. Our primary ministry is conducted through the spoken and sometimes written word, which will aid the Spirit of God to do His convicting work.

At each faith level on our spiritual journey, we can gladly say, as Paul did, about this potent ministry: "And I, brethren, when I came to you, did not come with excellence of speech or of wisdom declaring to you the testimony of God. For I determined not to know anything among you except Jesus Christ and Him crucified. I was with you in weakness, in fear, and in much trembling. And my speech and my preaching were not with persuasive words of human wisdom, but in demonstration of the Spirit and of power, that your faith should not be in the wisdom of men but in the power of God" (I Corinthians 2:1–5). Notice he wasn't depending on his abilities, but was serving on the basis that he was cooperating with God's Spirit in his ambassadorship.

Whether we desire it or not, to our circle of influence, we who call ourselves "Christian" are really ambassadors of the kingdom of God. Let us strive to be the best representatives we can be, for we are serving a royal and everlasting kingdom!

* * * * *

Prayer:

Dear Father God: It is awesome that You have called each of Your children to be Your ambassadors. Grant that I may study to show myself approved for this responsible privilege. In Jesus' name, I thank You that You have told us that Your Holy Spirit will teach us and reveal everything we need to proclaim Jesus as both Savior and Lord to a hurting and lost world. Amen.

CHAPTER 20

Appropriate God's Grace Through Suffering

∞

*For to you it has been granted on behalf of Christ,
not only to believe in Him, but also to suffer
for His sake.
(Philippians 1:29)*

Again we come to an important element of the believer's experience. It is rarely a part of our introduction to the Christian life. It is vital that we have a clear understanding of the universal occurrence of suffering for the children of God so that we will not waste the hidden purposes in what the Apostle Peter called "fiery trials which try us." He assures us that when these trying times happen, we can even "rejoice to the extent that you partake of Christ's sufferings" (I Peter 4:13).

The topic of suffering is a recurring subject throughout the Bible. We can be encouraged by the fact that whenever it is mentioned, the Scripture text usually speaks of a valuable reward to be gained when experiencing an unwanted episode, whether physical, mental, or emotional. Paul refers to this in II Thessalonians 1:3–6 as he relates to the early believers growing in faith and love toward one another. Here he couples these two spiritual characteristics with patience in enduring persecutions and tribulations. He explains that standing up to adverse circumstances is actually evidence of the righteous judgment of God. He allows His children to know suffering that they "may be counted worthy of the kingdom of God, for which you also suffer" (v. 5).

We usually don't learn the hard lessons of life apart from the misery that is involved. Christian history gives us ample magnificent examples of the full scope of suffering saints. We can always find many excellent qualities in those who have been honed and refined in the furnace of affliction. The admirable personalities of such twentieth-century Christian heroes as Corrie ten Boom and Watchman Nee were molded in the harsh cauldrons of severe hardship and human misunderstandings. Their lives and writings continue to testify to the blessed values of their single-minded determination to do God's will, even as they each spent much time in dirty prison compounds.

The gospel accounts of the sufferings of our Lord Jesus during His earthly ministry, which culminated on Calvary's cruel cross, convey the zenith of unjust agony. His steadfast attitude should be our pattern for dealing with whatever lesser adversities come into our lives. It is valuable to note that in the prophetic twenty-second Psalm, the description of the sufferings of Christ, that He endured with the trusting expressions of his praise to the Father. He was unwavering as He surrendered to the astonishing crucifixion that His Father required for our salvation.

For our immediate consideration, we will group the believer's sufferings into two distinct categories: those that are counted for the cause of Christ and the gospel, and the human miseries common to all humanity. The question of why godly people have to endure sickness, accidents, or physical and emotional abuse is shrouded in a mystery beyond our human ability to always understand or explain. We certainly cannot always generalize a cause either, but on one truth we can stand—God's Word always gives us the assurance that our loving heavenly Father is aware of our every circumstance. None of our painful experiences are wasted in His providence. When we stand on the promise of Romans 8:28, "that all things work together for good to those who love God, to those who are the called according to His purpose," we are fortified with an added ability to withstand hard tests and trials.

Christian suffering has been called the highway to perfection. We can be greatly consoled by the passage in I Peter 2, which assures believers that when enduring the grief of suffering unjustly, it is commendable before God. It is one of the essentials for qualifying to reign in our lives both now and in the age ahead with Christ, which both Peter and Paul refer to in their epistles.

A very reasonable observation has been made about one of the most important ways in which God has given His children to be used in the area of witnessing their faith. It is to simply live with the reality of whatever they are facing that can't be changed. Our Christian testimony is most impressive when we are able to stand in the midst of our trials. We are often unknowingly giving others the ability to bear their own ordeals.

We want to center in on the category of suffering for the Lord's sake, which is the main emphasis of today's text. The apostle James reminds us to "take the prophets, who spoke in the name of the Lord, as an example of suffering and patience" (James 5:10). We can count on the fact that whenever we speak from a biblical position, we will often have various degrees of opposition. Those who are walking in spiritual darkness by choice may react because they do not want to consider the consequences of their rebellion to truth. The atheist, who says he does not believe in God and displays animosity toward anything Christian, is really directing his anger toward God, not us.

We have Jesus as our example, and we are called to follow in His steps. The Holy Spirit can be relied on to give us wisdom in our spiritual encounters if we seek Him and pray to that end. We are maturing in faith when we do not respond emotionally in the face of suffering because of our witness. We are enabled to walk in the Spirit when we have our minds renewed by the unchangeable laws and promises of God's Word.

Most of us have not suffered great hostilities for our witness or have resisted to bloodshed by striving against sin as spoken of in Hebrews 11 and 12. But even in the face of that kind of traumatic situation, we are still exhorted to call on and look to Jesus, the author and finisher of our faith (Hebrews 12:2–4).

So much is written about suffering in the Bible that we can only touch on some of the many surprising benefits promised to us. We are told that when we suffer for the cause of Christ and the gospel, we are not only blessed and are given God's grace, but the Spirit of God and His glory rest upon us. Believers who are willing to participate in the arena of active faith are identifying themselves with the Godhead and are also assured that they are heirs of God and joint heirs with Jesus Christ. The opportunity to suffer with Him makes possible the privilege to also be glorified with Him.

Listen to this lovely benediction to a short meditation on suffering found in I Peter 5: "But may the God of all grace, who called us to His eternal glory by Christ Jesus, after you have suffered a while, perfect, establish, strengthen, and settle you. To Him be the glory and the dominion forever and ever. Amen" (vv. 10–11).

* * * * *

Prayer:
Dear heavenly Father: Only You can teach me how to endure in my appointments with suffering. Your Word assures me that when I do good and suffer for it and also take it patiently, it is commendable in Your eyes. Because Jesus suffered for me, beyond my ability to comprehend, He leaves me with an awesome example. Make me able to follow all the way for Jesus' sake. Amen.

CHAPTER 21

Appropriate Your Intercessor Role

∞

Therefore I exhort first of all that supplications,
prayers, intercessions,
and giving of thanks be made for all men,
for kings and all who are in authority,
that we may lead a quiet and peaceable life in all
godliness and reverence.
For this is good and acceptable in the sight of God
our Savior.
(I Timothy 2:1–3)

Do you keep a prayer journal? This is an excellent way for you to motivate yourself to respond to God's continual call for intercessors. As we keep personal records of answers to specific prayers for ourselves and others, our desire to earnestly intercede for others is greatly increased. The role of an intercessor is a very high calling. It is an invisible ministry that knows no limitations. The oldest, frailest saint who can no longer move about easily can still operate in the power of God at any hour of the day or night as he petitions God for others' needs.

We are reminded often in the gospel accounts that Jesus began His power ministry in prayer and that it continued to be His highest priority. This provides us with the meaning of a puzzling challenge, to "pray without ceasing." This is the attitude that Jesus displayed of always being in a state of open communication with His heavenly Father.

As we respond to the Holy Spirit's urgings to pray for others, we should be encouraged that we usually are not praying alone, or without spiritual fortification. Romans 8:26 and 27 assures believers that the Spirit Himself is now interceding for us. Jesus Christ, our High Priest of the New Covenant, is also at the Father's side, petitioning for His own beloved earthly family. "Therefore He is also able to save to the uttermost those who come to God through Him, since He always lives to make intercession for them," states Hebrews 7:25. We are joining our mortal petitions to divine prayer power.

We are exhorted to "pray always with all prayer and supplication in the Spirit" in the same portion of Ephesians 6 that we are told to "put on the whole armor of God." Remember we learned that prayer is a vital part of our God-given equipment. Just as we become skilled in effectively operating from within our uniform of spiritual protection, we will also gain skill in our spiritual tool of intercessory prayer.

This generation of praying Christians is still rallying around the challenge found in II Chronicles

7:14: "If My people who are called by My name will humble themselves, and pray and seek My face, and turn from their wicked ways, then I will hear from heaven, and will forgive their sin and heal their land." This gives us our first step in effectiveness. We come to God in a repentant attitude for ourselves and for those we pray for. We acknowledge the great mercies that we have been shown and that we are now seeking. Daniel's prayer as he interceded for his exiled countrymen gives us a good example (see Daniel 9:3–19).

The more of God's Word that we know, the more fluent our prayers will be. What is more potent than praying the Word of God back to Him? We are reminding our Father of His scriptural promises that apply to our prayer focus. We petition Him, not in an arrogant or presumptuous manner, but with a humble yet positive spirit. We must remember that we are His workmanship, and His Spirit will work in and through us as we take on the responsibility of prayer.

It is enlightening to learn what others before us have seen happen through intercession. Many people have testified that they were healed as they prayed for others. James 5:16–18 records this New Testament principle while referring to Elijah, a great Old Testament intercessor.

Although we do not really understand why the almighty God of the universe calls upon mere mortals to pray, He has ordained that His purposes will be accomplished when His people intercede. In view of the many needy situations all around us, there is no doubt that God is still seeking dedicated prayer warriors. We will do well to have the zeal of Daniel who cried, "O my God, incline Your ear and hear; open Your eyes and see our desolations, and the city which is called by Your name; for we do not present our supplications before You because of our righteous deeds, but because of Your great mercies" (Daniel 9:18). Today we have so much more than Daniel was aware. We have the indwelling of God's Holy Spirit to direct us, and we have been gifted with the righteousness of Christ as our qualifier.

What are we to be praying for after we follow the order of our chapter text? The salvation of the lost, the healing of sick souls and bodies, and that those who walk in darkness will have their eyes opened to their spiritual condition. Jesus meant for His people to tear down satanic strongholds through prayer. We can pray for people to be delivered from whatever binds them. We can pray that we and other believers will have a hunger for God's Word, and that we may all daily seek His will. When we become sensitized to this prayer dimension, God's Spirit will supply the focus.

We can learn to be bold in our intercessions as we study the prophets and apostles before us. They stood in the gap for the needs of others and saw mighty answers to their prayers. We can also turn inopportune times into precious moments of fruitful opportunities to entreat God on behalf of others. Have you ever felt an impression to pray at a traffic stop for someone in your line of vision? Maybe one day in the future, you will know what transpired because you were obedient to pray. Even distressful episodes of insomnia can be changed into consecrated midnight watches of intercession. Change your fretting into fruitfulness.

The men and women of the present-day body of Christ must fully realize that we are a part of a holy priesthood. We are meant to offer up spiritual, sacrificial prayers, acceptable to God through Jesus Christ. We will then see great and visible changes come about. Peter said that we could even *hasten the day* of our Lord's return. Oh, glory!

* * * * *

Prayer:

Dear Father God: Your Word tells me that Your Holy Spirit will teach me how to pray and even intercede for me as I pray. In the precious name of Jesus, I ask that You give me the heart of an intercessor; I already see so many needs in the world. Amen.

CHAPTER 22

Appropriate Your Teaching Role

∞

A servant of the Lord must not quarrel but
be gentle to all,
able to teach, patient, in humility correcting those
who are in opposition,
if God perhaps will grant them repentance, so that
they may know the truth.
(II Timothy 2:24–25)

In the course of our Christian lives, we will find many opportunities to appropriate the role of teacher of Bible truth. Many times this will occur in a most unplanned manner as chance occasions for our witness open up. Even the most shy and reserved believer can share the fundamentals of salvation on a one-to-one basis. We need to remember that being a witness for Jesus Christ is really informing others in His truth. This is God's intention for His followers, and it is pleasing to Him.

The Great Commission is the pivotal premise that all believers are meant to become able instructors of the gospel message's good news. A review of First and Second Timothy conveys Paul's Holy Spirit-inspired discourses about presenting sound doctrine. He called teaching "godly edification," and later declared that by this means one would be able to reject the profane and even old wives' tales. Scriptural truth is to displace senseless, worldly superstitions.

I Timothy 4 is a very timely and relevant study portion for all sincere followers of Jesus to heed. It could almost have been written for the present generation. Starting out by prophesying of the very deceptions still around us today, Paul gives clear instructions to all who would be "a good minister of Jesus Christ, nourished in the words of faith and of the good doctrine" (v. 6). We are further urged to be examples in both word and conduct as well as in love, spirit, faith, and purity. We are also to give dedicated attention to learning true scriptural doctrine. We are to encourage others to also embrace these things.

Listen to this epistle's admonition, which has a definite promise for the obedient: "Do not neglect the gift that is in you. . . . Meditate on these things . . . give yourself entirely to them, that your progress may be evident to all. Take heed to yourself and to the doctrine. Continue in them, for in doing this you will save both yourself and those who hear you" (vv. 14–16).

What is more natural than for parents to begin teaching their children the important value systems within months of birth? Although every youngster will need many categories of knowledge imparted to him to succeed in life, none will be as important or eternal as the early acceptance of the reality of his Creator God, and then being lovingly encouraged to personally receive His Son, Jesus Christ, as his Savior *and* Lord.

What a blessing and a challenge it is to volunteer to teach a Sunday school class. Have you ever considered how scriptural instruction received by one person continues on and can multiply from generation to generation? One of the many benefits of tutoring others in God's Word is that the teacher is also being saturated and reinforced with the rich promises, principles, and provisions that our Father has decreed for His children.

We may never be called to teach, but opportunities to share will appear if we watch for them. We all have neighbors where we live or work where we can share our faith in a natural manner. While we keep in mind that an employer has the right to expect his employees to be about company business during the work day, our sharing can be done on breaks with those who are open to us.

Many people all around us have life problems that can be dealt with only when they make Jesus their Lord. In one-to-one witnessing, we are being good stewards of our ministry gifts and the manifold grace of God.

We have stated in previous chapters that Jesus is our pattern for living the abundant life. We can go to the four gospels and study His ministry methods. In addition to teaching in the formal setting of a synagogue, He more often gave spiritual instructions in spontaneous and natural surroundings—at the seashore, in rural locations, and while walking down country roads. This is how many of our chances to "always be ready to give a defense to everyone who asks you a reason for the hope that is in you" will happen (see I Peter 3:15).

It is never necessary to "collar" someone to share our faith. In actuality, probably only a small percentage of forceful or inappropriate witnessing has positive results. In many cases, negative or resentful feelings may linger long after an insensitive approach.

Jesus never cornered people; they came to Him! We can rely on the Holy Spirit to put us in contact with those He is drawing. The joy of nurturing others who are open to the Scriptures is priceless. We can share in their delight as they are presented with Spirit-anointed principles for living that illuminate their understanding. Then it is the Spirit Himself who will draw them to know Jesus Christ as their Savior, Lord, and baptizer.

* * * * *

Prayer:

Dear heavenly Father: As I see so many people walking in darkness, I don't want to miss the blessedness of sharing my faith as a teacher of Your truth. Like the plea of Psalm 19:14, "Let the words of my mouth and the meditation of my heart be acceptable in Your sight, O Lord, my strength and my Redeemer." Lead me to someone who is ready to hear the good news of the gospel message. I rely on Your Holy Spirit. In Jesus' name I pray. Amen.

CHAPTER 23

Appropriate Your Role as a Comforter

∞

Blessed be the God and Father of our Lord
Jesus Christ,
the Father of mercies and God of all comfort,
who comforts us in all our tribulation,
that we may be able to comfort those who are in
any trouble,
with the comfort with which we ourselves are
comforted by God.
(II Corinthians 1:3–4)

This rich text promise brings to mind some of the many unsettling instances when we have been comforted by the God of *all* comfort. Often we remember those who have conveyed comfort to us. They gave us a steadying hope by directing our thoughts away from our stress and back to Jesus, our abiding Savior and beloved Shepherd.

We may feel unqualified to appropriate the role of

God's comforter, but more than likely we have already done this, often without realizing it. The very fact that God's Spirit and His Word have taken us through the turmoil of some troubling episodes causes us to want to offer hope to others. Hope is the first positive thing we can offer to someone suffering in distressing circumstances. Romans 15:13 states: "Now may the God of hope fill you with all joy and peace in believing, that you may abound in hope by the power of the Holy Spirit."

The second effective knowledge we can share with those who seek our counsel is the truth of God's Holy Scriptures. What God has said is more important and useful than anything that man can advise. We need not overwhelm them with a multitude of Bible verses. If we have been faithful to invest our time in studying the Bible, we can rely on the Spirit of God to give us just the right verses. We can then rest in the divine ability of His Spirit's anointing on His Word to minister to them directly. How reassuring it is to recall that "the word of God is living and powerful, and sharper than any two-edged sword, piercing even to the division of soul and spirit, and of joints and marrow, and is a discerner of the thoughts and intents of the heart" Hebrews 4:12).

We have already discussed in past chapters that Jesus dwells in all believers and we are to reckon ourselves "in Christ." Since one of His many names is Wonderful Counselor (Isaiah 9:6), we have the potential to give some basic help to those who ask. Part of that help may be to direct them to professional Spirit-baptized counselors. To direct them to secular professionals will never totally resolve their problems. Secular counselors have been trained to deal only with the soul of man, but usually spiritual factors need to be addressed which are beyond their understanding.

It is painful to watch friends whose lives are almost at a standstill because of troubling dilemmas. Whether or not we know exactly what they should do, the Lord desires that we voice our assurance that they will be able to either resolve their situations or find suitable ways to live in the peace of God while their conditions exist. It may be that they need to be reminded that making Jesus Lord of their lives will be their greatest stabilizing force. Eventually they should come to understand that they are meant to seek the mind of Christ for themselves day by day.

A professional Christian counselor has wisely advised that as we listen with loving compassion to others as they describe their problems, they will come no closer to resolving them if nothing else transpires. Biblically based counselors not only endeavor to give hope but also offer scriptural instruction for dealing with the situations. The counselors are reinforced by the knowledge that when biblical principles are applied, they have seen healings of the spirit, soul, body, and even fractured relationships.

We also must urge them to be diligent in applying the principles of God's Word to their situations as long as necessary. James 1:22 states: "Be doers of the word, and not hearers only, deceiving yourselves." When they are already seeking qualified biblical help, we should encourage them to follow the scriptural instructions from their counselors.

After we share hope through the Word of God and emphasize the lordship of Christ in the circumstances, we will want to pray with them. They can be further encouraged if we write out the texts or complete verses that we have shared. When they are impressed with the value of memorizing and meditating on the Scriptures they are to believe in and act on, they will see their faith and peace increase.

There are times when we will recognize that some people like to merely talk about their problems but have no intentions of taking any positive steps for change. When this is evident, we eventually have to confront them and remind them that we aren't offering to be just "dump sites." Listening to problems is not only wearisome at times, but it can also eat up hours that the Lord may want us to invest in other ways. This is a matter for prayer and discernment of the Spirit.

As we are willing to be available vessels for the therapy of the Holy Spirit, we will often be blessed as we see works of real regeneration in others' lives. Our part is to be whole ourselves, committed to give of our time and energy, and to be aware of our own limitations. It means showing the compassion of Christ as we personally have enjoyed Him. Our attitude must be supportive but not superior. Once again, we are reminded that we are His ministers of reconciliation. Proverbs 18:4 says: "The words of a man's mouth are deep waters; the wellspring of wisdom is a flowing brook."

* * * * *

Prayer:

Dear Father God: As I have the opportunity to testify that Jesus is the only lasting answer for those who are seeking aid and comfort in their dilemmas, may I be filled and led by Your Holy Spirit. In Jesus' name, I pray for wisdom, compassion, and discernment of Your will in the encounters. Amen.

CHAPTER 24

Appropriate Your Healing Role

∽

Most assuredly, I say to you, he who believes in Me,
the works that I do he will do also;
and greater works than these he will do,
because I go to My Father.
And whatever you ask in My name, that I will do,
that the Father may be glorified in the Son.
(John 14:12–13)

And these signs will follow those who believe:
In My name they will cast out demons; they will
speak with new tongues;
they will take up serpents;
and if they drink anything deadly, it will by no
means hurt them;
they will lay hands on the sick, and they will
recover.
(Mark 16:17–18)

As Christ's ambassadors, we have His assurance that we are to proclaim the healing Jesus to those who are afflicted. The timeless truth of Hebrews 13:8, which says that "Jesus Christ is the same yesterday, today, and forever," is our New Testament guarantee that we are to direct our prayer petitions to Him on behalf of the ill.

We have already looked into the spiritual endowment of our own wholeness in chapter four. The same scriptural principles listed there are to be shared with fellow believers. It is our continual expectation to be seeking a greater degree of wholeness as we yield to "Christ in us, the hope of glory" (see Colossians 1:27).

While we recognize the valid ministries of pastors, elders, and Christian professionals in the ministry of healing, God honors the concern of every believer who will pray for and encourage the sick. Just as Jesus walked in the ministry of compassion, His Spirit now desires to bring wholeness through His body of believers today.

Believers can extend the healing ministry of Jesus in many ways as we are sensitive to the leading of the Holy Spirit. All around us are people with physical and emotional afflictions that we can lift to God in the prayer of faith. We do not need to be professional counselors to give hope to others, according to our two theme texts. When we ask to pray for their needs, we are extending hope to them. And it is very rare to have our offers to pray refused, even for unbelievers.

When we previously discussed wholeness, we submitted the fact that in addition to the need of physical healing, people can just as often need the Lord's restoration of their emotions or of broken relationships.

Compassion for people is real evidence that the fruit of the Holy Spirit has been activated in our lives. Having knowledge of the Word of God is the basis for being able to minister to those who need healing. That does not mean that we are to flood them with all the healing Scriptures. Less is often more when directed toward those whose minds are already over-burdened by their predicaments. We need to be alert to what God wants to do at the moment. Let His Spirit bring to your remembrance several strong verses that they can grasp. Encourage and direct them to specific portions of the Bible that they can read for themselves. This will increase their faith.

In dealing with lengthy illnesses, there can be several hindrances to those needing healing. They include disbelief, fear, or a need of repentance. The Word of God can drive out the fear and doubt that often block the afflicted from receiving deliverance from their troubles. The Scriptures can also bring them to an understanding of the need to ask God for forgiveness and to forgive others. It is simply a matter of bringing them to recognize this principle and then offering to lead them in prayers of repentance before praying for healing.

We do not want to feel rushed through these times of ministry. If this happens, it is well to take our authority over this harassing spirit in the name of Jesus. Whether we do this vocally or by silently praying in the Spirit, we rely on the day's text. We have been given the scriptural keys to God's kingdom with the right to bind any hindering spirits that are opposing the light of the gospel message of hope (see Matthew 16:19 and Ephesians 6:10–18).

When we have opportunities to minister, we can join our faith with the faith of God. We are not dependent on those we are praying for to have a certain level of faith. While it is valuable to know that they have a measure of faith, we who pray are standing in agreement with the promises of God and are depending on His sovereign power and mercy.

God created the universe with His spoken words. Words still have power today. We have all experienced the power of words to hurt or to bless us. As believers, we need to learn how to speak in a positive life-giving manner. It causes people to grasp hope and to appropriate the healing virtue that Jesus readily offers.

The glory of God is displayed when people are healed. It brings a reality that He is God of the "now." All sincere believers can be compassionate vessels for the Spirit of God to extend the healing virtue of Jesus Christ. Our part is to make ourselves available and to study the Scriptures in preparation.

A wise teacher said that we believers might err in understanding our spiritual potential. When we have no expectation of being used of God, we don't prepare, and when opportunities come, we are not ready. Although we live in a time of advancing medical knowledge and an enlightened awareness of good health measures, all around us many people are sick in body, soul, or spirit. Let us be about our Father's business in whatever arena He desires to proclaim His healing love.

* * * * *

Prayer:

Dear Father God: Thank You that You have provided me with wholeness through the salvation of Jesus. In His name I pray that You will use me to bring Your healing promises to my family and others. Give me opportunities with those that my life touches to share Your healing love in the mighty name of Jesus. Amen.

CHAPTER 25

Appropriate Your Role as God's Deliverer

∞

For the weapons of our warfare are not carnal but mighty in God for pulling down strongholds.
(II Corinthians 10:4)

One of the names of Jesus is Deliverer. Romans 11:26 states: "The Deliverer will come out of Zion, and He will turn away ungodliness from Jacob." Every time Jesus commanded evil spirits out of the lives of the afflicted and bound, He was turning away ungodliness. Surely when we see people bound and we discern by the Holy Spirit that they are captive, we cannot turn away and still be operating in God's kind of love. We must help or get help! Our first priority is to pray for God's guidance.

In each of these previous chapters, we have learned that our heavenly Father has invested His faith and love in us, His children. Through the atonement of Jesus Christ, God has endowed us with the

143

same righteous authority that Jesus displayed to act on His behalf here and now. The foremost characteristic of His earthly ministry was delivering people from the bonds of darkness, demons, and infirmities. "He [God the Father] has delivered us from the power of darkness and conveyed us into the kingdom of the Son of His love," declares Colossians 1:13. Jesus acted aggressively against the kingdom of Satan.

As we meditate on today's theme text, the basic question to consider is whether we will appropriate the weapons of our spiritual warfare with the same authority that Jesus gave to His first disciples. Those who avoid this needed responsibility are settling for passive and ineffective roles instead of being the dedicated soldiers of the cross that the Lord intends.

Let us review the original standing orders that Jesus personally laid out for His sincere disciples. "And when He had called His twelve disciples to Him, He gave them power over unclean spirits, to cast them out, and to heal all kinds of sickness and all kinds of disease" (Matthew 10:1). The fact that Jesus called His disciples "to Himself" can be a vital key phrase to motivate us. The Spirit of Christ has called every born-again believer out of darkness and into the light of His salvation.

When we sincerely choose to make Jesus the Lord of our lives, His righteousness qualifies us to not only learn about Him but also to learn to walk as He walked. His declared assignment from His Father was this: "He has anointed Me to preach the gospel to the poor; He has sent Me to heal the broken-hearted, to proclaim liberty to the captives and recovery of sight to the blind, to set at liberty those who are oppressed; to proclaim the acceptable year of the Lord" (Luke 4:18–19). This is also meant to be the disciple's God-ordained testimony and assigned purpose.

The entire Bible is a record of ongoing spiritual warfare. We are meant to share the powerful Word of God with people who will listen, and then expect to see freeing changes occur. Our first priority as God's deliverers is to give witness to the gospel message: salvation comes through believing that Jesus Christ can deliver people from the darkness in their souls because He is the light of the world!

The New Testament contains a wealth of specific instructions for our success as God's deliverers, of which only a few can be covered here. Let us look at some scriptural basics. "Put on the whole armor of God, that you may be able to stand against the wiles of the devil." (See Ephesians 6:10–18 and refer to chapter 13 of this book.) Our righteous equipment for bringing about God's rule in a situation and seeing people set free from bondage has been adequately provided for and ordained by God. We always proclaim the Word of God and the name of Jesus Christ in the power of His might.

The effective believer is a Christ-centered, Spirit- and Word-equipped minister. We are to continuously ask God for His power to clothe us. All known sins in our lives are to be confessed and stated as being under the cleansing blood of the Lamb. Here is where the ministry gifts of discernment, faith, and knowledge are necessary. (See I Corinthians 12 and chapter 4 of this book.)

This is a serious ministry. It is best learned by observing mature believers who are seasoned in dealing with people who desire to be set free from their personal captivity. By accompanying believers who are serving in this way, we can learn the scriptural mode of ministering. Many Christians and unbelievers are bound and hampered from enjoying life because of health-destroying habits and erroneous thought patterns. They can be helped and changed by the Spirit of the living God.

When God brings people across our paths who need to be miraculously touched by Him, He is very able to deliver them through His willing servants. The responsibility for the total dismantling of Satan's evil domain is assigned to Christ and His followers, both in the church age and the age to come. We need to believe Jesus when He said that if we believe in Him, the works that He did, we would do also (see John 14:12).

Space does not allow for expounding on the many New Testament Scriptures that contain instructions on this valid and needed ministry. We can be alert to the Holy Spirit's edification as we read the New Testament. He will increase our faith and knowledge. He will also deliver us from fear and timidity. We have been charged with the power and the promises of Jesus. Our part is to put faith into action. When we become sensitive to what God's Spirit is saying to our spirits, He will lead us to those who will be open to our help.

* * * * *

Prayer:

Dear heavenly Father: You brought me out of great darkness and a bondage to my ignorance. In the power and authority of Jesus' name, I pray for the wisdom and ability to minister to others who I see living so far below Your rich provisions. Fill me with Your Holy Spirit and give me a continual hunger for Your Word, that I may be a servant of Your deliverance. Amen.

CHAPTER 26

Appropriate Your Watchman Role

∞

*Praying always with all prayer and supplication
in the Spirit, being watchful to this end
with all perseverance and supplication
for all the saints.
(Ephesians 6:18)*

God has always had watchmen, sentries for warning and protecting His people. With the same consistency that we are given the biblical message to "hear," we also have the call to "watch." It makes for an interesting topical study to research the numerous Scriptures that refer to our watchman role.

What are we to watch for, you ask? First of all, we are to keep a watch on ourselves—both our reactions and our endeavors. We know that when we call ourselves Christians, the world is observing to see how we live and if we stumble in our walk of faith.

Early in the Old Testament, we have the record of

God warning the people to be watchful. Exodus 23:13 states, "And in all that I have said to you, be circumspect and make no mention of the name of other gods, nor let it be heard from your mouth." Later the Psalmist affirms, "I will guard my ways, lest I sin with my tongue" (Psalm 39:1).

God's watchmen are prayer warriors. It will require our discernment to be aware of the occasions we are called to this hidden ministry. When we become alerted to someone in an acute situation, we need to be quick to pray for him, even if the full particulars are not revealed. We can present his cause to the Father, in the name of Jesus, anticipating the help of His Spirit. Other times we may be impressed to bind specific spiritual forces in the name of Jesus that could be operating in the situation (see Matthew 16:18–19).

Jesus admonished His disciples to watch and pray, and at the same time they were to heed their own actions. We do well to remember the divine principle that we will not have an open line to our heavenly Father when we are in need of repentant confession of any hindering sin (see Mark 11:25–26).

Jesus told Peter to feed and care for the lambs and sheep. We realize He was not talking about livestock. He was reminding Peter and all believers that the young among us always need special watch care and nurturing until they are established in the faith. As members of local fellowships, we who are mindful of our watchman role will be standing alongside new believers with both our encouragement and prayers.

It can be readily noted that the word "heed" is often used in many of the Old and New Testament texts about being watchful. The person who heeds instructions or circumstances is one who gives his careful attention. The good watchman has the characteristics of being observant, protective, and alert. We are to heed our Lord's directives and warnings at all times and be ready and willing to caution others.

We are living in a time that is high in the expectancy of the nearing return of Jesus Christ to planet earth. All around us in the Christian world, many voices are projecting their estimation of the timing of "last day" Bible prophecies. What should be our stance in view of the wide range of speculations? We cannot include all the specific gospel instructions that Jesus gave on this matter, but it is of great value to be alert to His teachings and give them the highest validity. Review Matthew 24 and Luke 17 for His instructions. We must make the studying of God's Word our daily "bread" so that we will know and recognize the signs of the times that Jesus told His disciples would occur before He could return to set up His kingdom.

Chapter 13 of the gospel of Mark is a fruitful portion relating to those who desire to claim the blessings of the "latter day" praying watchmen. They will be able to abide in the peace and restful assurance of the Lord's perfect timing. That chapter concluded with Jesus saying this: "But of that day and hour no one knows, not even the angels in heaven, nor the Son, but only the Father. Take heed, watch and pray; for you do not know when the time is. . . . Watch therefore, for you do not know when the master of the house is coming . . . lest, coming suddenly, he find you sleeping. And what I say to you, I say to all: Watch!" (vv. 32, 33, 35–37). This is a command to all true disciples.

Today's theme text contains the essence of our watchman mandate. It is that of being concerned about and alerting people to the lateness of the hour. We are to use our spiritual endowments and authority to pray and seek God's reign of righteousness over needy situations in obedience to Jesus, our Supreme Commander.

* * * * *

Prayer:

Dear Father God: We can waste precious time in wondering just when and how this age will end. It causes confusion and sometimes even divisions in the Christian family. I can sense that this is not pleasing to You. I praise and thank You that there is great peace in trusting in Your wisdom and providential timing. Help me to be Your watchman to my world. In Jesus' name I ask this. Amen.

CHAPTER 27

Appropriate Your Peacemaker Role

∞

Blessed are the peacemakers, for they shall be called sons of God.
(Matthew 5:9)

Counselors of peace have joy.
(Proverbs 12:20b)

Have you ever been with certain Christians who seem to have an evident spirit of peace about them? Just being with them can add a dimension of tranquility to your day. These individuals have the spiritual fruit of peace fully developed in their lives. They have believed deeply in the promise of peace that Jesus bestowed on His disciples. His peace, which truly is beyond understanding, is the inheritance of all believers.

In this fast-paced world, where stress seems to be a predominate factor in so many endeavors, being able to appropriate the biblical peace that we are repeatedly promised is a marvelous endowment. It is an advantage or edge that gives solid tranquility to our lives. We can operate in a state of mind that enables God to readily call upon us to act as His peacemakers.

To qualify for this service, we must learn to walk in peace at all times in spite of any distressing conditions that come into our lives. Stress, the opposite of peace, is a great robber of our mental and physical energy. Too much stress at any time can almost paralyze our best reactions. Satan, God's enemy and ours, knows that he can put a stop to our effective Christian witness and service if he can cause our lives to be stressfully unbalanced or self-centered.

Shortly before Jesus concluded His earthly ministry instructions, He told the disciples that He was bestowing the precious gift of peace on them (see John 14:27). When we read this rich portion of Scripture, we take the balance of these instructions as being meant for all generations of believers. But do we consistently appropriate His blessed peace and the vital qualities it provides for our daily lives? It takes some disciplined self-training to establish the spiritual fruit of peace firmly in our makeup. This is one of the real values of memorizing and meditating on Scripture verses. It has permanent and essential benefits.

Several New Testament principles conclude with the specific promise of peace as a reward for our obedience. Two primary examples are found in Philippians 4:6–7: "Be anxious for nothing, but in everything by prayer and supplication, with thanksgiving, let your requests be made known to God; and the peace of God, which surpasses all understanding, will guard your hearts and minds through Christ Jesus."

In other words, when we can't handle a situation, or even cope with just riding it out, we are to throw the whole thing on the lordship of Christ. Then with a grateful heart, we are to wait for, and even expect, His instructions and the compassionate providence of God. Peace is our operating mode.

In Philippians 4:8, the Apostle Paul explains the positive and beneficial actions we are to take that will ensure an unshakable peace in the midst of life's troubles: "Finally, brethren, whatever things are true, whatever things are noble, whatever things are just, whatever things are pure, whatever things are lovely, whatever things are of good report, if there is any virtue and if there is anything praiseworthy—meditate on these things." I believe the Holy Spirit through Paul is saying that we are to focus our thoughts on finding any one of these eight positives as we are determined to appropriate and walk in God's peace.

We are to accentuate the positive, giving contemplative thought to the unchangeable absolutes in our lives. At times this may give us reason we could confront Paul and say, "Oh, sure, Paul, that was easy for you to write, but you don't know what unbearable things I'm dealing with now!" But reading between the lines, Paul no doubt knew that these instructions would be hard to follow, for he added this footnote: "The things which you learned and received and heard and saw in me, these do, and the God of peace will be with you" (Philippians 4:9).

Paul's reference here is to the vast array of distressing experiences he had weathered since coming under the lordship of Jesus Christ. We can read about these stressful episodes in the book of Acts. He confirmed, through the inspiration of the Holy Spirit, that by following these tested procedures, God's peace did rest upon him. He had proof positive that allowed him to assure us that these formulas do work!

Those who minister as God's peacemakers have attractive and compelling dispositions. People like to be in their company. Even their enemies will be at peace with them, according to Proverbs 16:7. Being peacemakers does not mean we are to go about looking for people and situations that we can "straighten out." But when God's Spirit impresses us that we have the liberty to aid in restoring a fractured relationship, we will learn to mix boldness with discretion and to offer the applicable scriptural principles.

Have you not realized that whenever we witness about our Savior and Lord Jesus Christ, we are acting as God's peacemakers? Romans 10:15 states, "How beautiful are the feet of those who preach the gospel of peace, who bring glad tidings of good things!" What a joy it is to see a person invite Jesus to become his Savior, thereby becoming justified by faith, and begin to experience peace with God through His Son (see Romans 5:1). This is the zenith of our peacemaker role.

The spiritual fruit listed in Galatians 4:22, which every believer is to cultivate, enhances and gives much grace to our peacemaker role. Our part is to have the awareness to yield to God as He develops these godly and winsome characteristics of Jesus in us. They can mature more readily through the presence of genuine, unshakable peace.

* * * * *

Prayer:

Dear Father God: Thank You for Your sweet peace. I remember how much turmoil and unrest was in my life before I knew Jesus as my Savior and Lord. I want to be Your ambassador of peace to those around me. Help me not to be timid when I can speak words that might bring calmness to those in distressful situations. May You cause them to see Jesus as their source of peace, for it is in His name I ask. Amen.

CHAPTER 28

Appropriate Your Sonship Role

∞

For as many as are led by the Spirit of God,
these are sons of God.
For you did not receive the spirit of bondage
again to fear,
but you received the Spirit of adoption by whom we
cry out, "Abba, Father."
The Spirit Himself bears witness with our spirit
that we are children of God.
(Romans 8:14–16)

A puzzle is abroad in the land today. In some Christian circles, the term "sonship" causes a negative reaction. The thought of our appropriating spiritual sonship with God is held to be presumptuous. Yet the New Testament repeatedly relates to us that every born-again believer in Jesus Christ is now a child of God.

New believers are precious fruitful seed to the

Father. All the potentials of sonship reside in us at the time of our spiritual birth, but they are in the embryonic state. Just as each plant's seed requires water to begin germination to grow and attain its full development, we too must be watered by the nourishing Word of God on a regular basis for our complete and intended maturation.

Today's text declares the primary identifying characteristic of sons of the living God: they are "led by the Spirit of God." He provides every believer with the capability of receiving guidance from His Holy Spirit. This has been His standard operating procedure since Jesus returned to the heavenly Father's throne. This is a church-age, present-day relational provision.

Are we actively living in this blessed relationship to its fullest? Let us review some basic facts. When a child is born physically, he is instantly known as the offspring of a human mother and father. From the moment he draws his first breath, he is identified as the infant child of his natural parents.

Through the years, the child will encounter learning situations. With each new instruction, he may fail to learn at the initial attempt. But whether he fails or succeeds, he is still his parents' child. He was a baby, an adolescent, a teenager, and finally an adult offspring of his natural parents.

So it is with our spiritual relationship with God. We must all go through the stages of being spiritual babes, then adolescents, and then hopefully on to mature, adult sons of God. As the Spirit of God begins the teaching process, we often fail the lessons on the first or even the second and third tries. But we are still the children of God; He does not and will not disregard our relationship to Him because of our defeats and shortcomings. We can rest in this blessed confidence to be found reassuring believers throughout the Bible.

For example, believers learn to have the manifestations of spiritual gifts operate through them by first being made aware of the possibility and then staying alert to the Holy Spirit's impressions and timing. Even in the school of the Spirit, practice makes perfect. We are sons of God in this developmental maturation of our full potential. We can and must stand firmly on the truth of Hebrews 12:2 that Jesus Christ is the *author* and *finisher* of our faith journey. Our determined stance is to *never* give up!

To newly instructed believers, it begins as just head knowledge that they are children of the living God. The personal revelation is quickened and deepened for many when they allow Jesus to baptize them with or into His Holy Spirit. It is like the scales of spiritual blindness that were removed from the Apostle Paul's eyes at his baptism in the Spirit at the ministry of Ananias (Acts 9:17–18). When we request Jesus to baptize us with His Holy Spirit, our spiritual perception is greatly increased. We are enabled to receive spiritual knowledge at a deeper level. That is why we often observe such outward and joyous vitality in people who are newly filled with the Spirit. Their sonship relationship reality has been expanded and enlarged.

"Behold what manner of love the Father has bestowed on us, that we should be called children of God!" This is what we can declare along with the beloved Apostle John in I John 3:1. He goes on to affirm our present position by saying in verse two: "Beloved, now we are children of God; and it has not yet been revealed what we shall be, but we know that when He is revealed, we shall be like Him, for we shall see Him as He is."

The four gospels give us the manner in which Jesus displayed His obedience. The balance of the New Testament contains the full directions for developing the characteristics of Jesus, the pattern Son. We can also be greatly enlightened by studying the books of Psalms and Proverbs, for in these wisdom-filled books, we learn what pleases and displeases our heavenly Father.

A basic key verse to motivate us is I John 2:6, which states, "He who says he abides in Him ought himself also to walk just as He walked." When we really have the inner revelation that we are meant to appropriate the sonship that Jesus purchased for His followers, we will walk in awe. We should have a humble yet sure determination to seek the destiny that Almighty God holds out to each of His children.

As heirs of God and joint heirs with Jesus, we will desire to acquire that sensitivity to the Holy Spirit that precedes obedience to the divine commandments. There is an added bonus for some. For the believers whose earthy parents have forsaken them, accepting their heavenly relationship is a healing balm that allows resentment and unforgiveness to be completely dissolved.

The steps to sonship are clear and plain. We make it seem impossible because we look at our own limitations, but we attain this by being obedient to the

Scripture's truth and then acquiring a yielded attitude to the Spirit's promptings. Yes, there will be many tests and trials, but as believers, obedience is our means of learning to be overcomers and even experiencing God in the midst of all of them.

As we attend to the Word of God, we are being instructed in righteousness. The spiritual laws and commandments were given to all children of God to bring maturity and to help them reach their full potential. The development of the fruit of the Spirit will be a natural outflow of our obedience. In a surprised state of awe, we can humbly see the love, joy, peace, and other characteristics of Christ being activated in us for our relationships and ministry opportunities.

* * * * *

Prayer:

Dear heavenly Father: Thank You for claiming me as Your child. I rejoice in my eternal relationship with You, Father, and with Your Son and Holy Spirit. Deepen my understanding of what my sonship role is to be today as well as all my tomorrows. I treasure the truth that everyone who has the hope in Jesus purifies himself, just as He is pure.[5*] It is in His precious name I pray. Amen.

CHAPTER 29

Appropriate Your Rest in God

∞

There remains therefore a rest for the people
of God.
For he who has entered His rest has himself also
ceased from his works
as God did from His. Let us therefore be diligent
to enter that rest.
(Hebrews 4:9–11)

The true rest of God is not a day of the week. It is meant to be our spiritual abiding place. In each of the covenants that God has made with mankind, He has always provided a position of rest for those who would commit to His covenant requirements.

A quick reading of the chapter subtitles found throughout the book of Psalms conveys the repeated theme that believers are meant to begin appropriating the rest of God as soon as they perceive its availability. The awesome promise of Psalm 91:1 is that

"He who dwells in the secret place of the Most High shall abide under the shadow of the Almighty." That secret abiding place is found in verse nine for those who make the Lord their habitation.

Let us review just a few of the many scriptural statements that will encourage our entering more fully into God's present-day rest for His children. We know that our physical bodies require a repeated portion of each twenty-four-hour period in the sleep/rest state. When we are deprived from getting at least a minimum number of hours of quality rest and sleep, in a very short time we experience a definite depletion of our physical and mental reserves. We quickly cease to perform at our usual level of ability in every area of our daily functions and responsibilities.

As believers, we are meant to continually partake of the divine peace and rest that have been provided for our souls and spirits as well. The spiritual grace of rest is to be an uninterrupted constant for God's family members, not just a periodic happening.

The familiar promise of Matthew 11:28–29, which Jesus gave to His first disciples, is an excellent springboard for our meditation in learning to abide in the blessed tranquility of God-ordained rest. "Come to Me, all you who labor and are heavy laden, and I will give you rest. Take My yoke upon you and learn from Me, for I am gentle and lowly in heart, and you will find rest for your souls." Ah, what a comforting promise!

Once again, we are reminded that Jesus is our source. It is only by receiving from Him that we will start enjoying the true rest, which is to be found only in the Christian life. We come to understand that we can labor in God's vineyard and still abide in rest for our souls. It is in the realm of the soul that we worry, fret, and try to figure out tomorrow's problems. Our spirits do not worry or fret, but have been fashioned in the peace of God. Our minds and emotions are not fully trusting and leaning into God's yoke. The yoke has been specifically designed for each of us. It is part of our inheritance and destiny of being "in Christ." That's where we want to be, isn't it?

I know that some readers may think that our theme is implying that after converting to Christianity, we can just hang on to our "spiritual fire insurance" and loaf unaccountably through life, bypassing instructions for growth and responsibility. Any teaching on the grace of God without referring to seeking the overcoming life is only a half-truth and is injurious to both the teacher and the hearer. Believers are "works in progress."

Most of the chapter themes convey our position. This chapter is on entering God's rest as overcoming, maturing servants of the Most High God. We want to highlight the most peaceful stance available to each of us. We are examining the scriptural paradox of being vital, growing members of the body of Christ, learning to serve God and people from positions of rest and security in our spirits, hearts, and minds. We are to be strong in the grace that is in Christ Jesus according to II Timothy 2:1.

We can come to a sure understanding of what it means to enter God's rest by reading Hebrews 3 and 4. These two chapters should help us stay alert and yielded to God's purposes. There we learn of the primary attitude that kept the Israelites from entering God's rest. In that lengthy wilderness experience, God said that they went astray in their hearts and they would not know or learn His ways. They had hard, unteachable hearts and mindsets that produced the double sin of disobedience and doubting unbelief. Unbelief is still a very costly negative today. It is actually a spirit of rebellion and a well-used tool of our adversary, Satan. Peter reminded us that he is just waiting to entice the careless and the uncommitted (I Peter 5:8–9).

So what is to be our enlightened stance? How do we learn to walk in the yoke of the disciple while also enjoying this blessed godly rest that is part of the believer's present inheritance? The key element is to be our faithfulness to the commandments and the spiritual principles of God. They are all to be clearly found in His new covenant, which is the New Testament of the Holy Bible.

Our faith can be portrayed in three degrees. We start at the upright position when we believe in God. When we come to the point of personally acknowledging our need of a Savior, and in true repentance we ask Jesus into our lives, we can be pictured as beginning to lean toward the Godhead in faith. Then by diligently seeking to learn all we can about our heavenly Father, His Son, Jesus Christ, and His Holy Spirit, we find that we progress into a third position of repose. This is trust—leaning more and more into the everlasting arms of our Creator. Now we are appropriating His rest, while at the same time we are earnestly learning what is most pleasing to Him. It sounds like marriage, doesn't it? This is the disposition of those who will make up the bride of Christ. This is seeking your personal destiny.

Are you ready to lean further into your beloved Lord of Lords and King of Kings? It is our move; He is patiently waiting for our response to His loving invitation and intentions. Like the Apostle Paul, we can rest in this statement in Philippians 1:6: "being confident of this very thing, that He who has begun a good work in you will complete it until the day of Jesus Christ."

As we cultivate the truth that we are now "in Christ" and He is "in us," then we will begin to live with the double expectation of rest and maturing usefulness. In today's vernacular, we could label it "to go with the divine flow."

* * * * *

Prayer:

Dear Father God: Thank You that in this hectic world, You have provided for my resting in Your love. As I remember that Jesus is the author and finisher of my faith, I desire to yield more fully into the changes and growth You have in mind for me. In Jesus' name, I praise You for Your great patience and love. Amen.

CHAPTER 30

Appropriate the Divine Nature

∞

To those who have obtained like precious faith with
us by the righteousness of our God and
Savior Jesus Christ: Grace and peace be multiplied
to you in the knowledge of God
and of Jesus our Lord, as His divine power
has given to us all things that pertain to life and
godliness, through the knowledge of Him who
called us by glory and virtue, by which have been
given to us exceedingly great and precious
promises, that through these you may be partakers
of the divine nature, having escaped the corruption
that is in the world through lust.
(II Peter 1:1–4)

When we read these potent theme verses, stating that one of God's promises is to give each of us a divine nature, it staggers our imagination. We are apt, like Sarah of old, to laugh at the seeming impossibility of such a thing! We are well aware of our mortal, human condition. At the first reading of these Scriptures, we may feel presumptuous to consider that such a change could even begin this side of eternity. Even so, let us examine this New Testament proclamation closely, lest we carelessly dismiss it like hidden treasure that can be passed over. For though Peter had recorded the promises, we need to remember that he was being inspired by God's Spirit.

Here we have Peter, one of God's apostles and scribes, conveying to fellow believers a valid part of God's new covenant or contract with His earthly family. It is a statement of some of the precious spiritual endowments that we still have available for our appropriation during our Christian lifetime.

Point one: The scriptural promise is directed to those who *have obtained* the similar valuable faith with Peter (v. 1) by the righteousness of God. An active faith in God and His Word is our first qualifier that leads us to expect changes in our present nature, which comprises the character, temperament, and personality.

Point two: Peter writes that he expects grace and peace to be multiplied to us as we gain knowledge of God the Father and Jesus our Lord (v. 2). We can become acquainted with the divine nature of God only by reading the Bible and through our growing relationship with the triune Godhead: Father, Son, and Holy Spirit. The Old and New Testaments not only contain the record of God's merciful and just dealings with mankind, but as we have been surveying in these meditations, they contain innumerable commandments and specific directions to each believer.

We learn of God's divine nature as it was directed toward people from the historical record. But more personally, we come to understand the divine nature on the realistic basis as we commune with Him in prayer. We will identify the godly characteristics through His ongoing interaction with our lives. As we become intimately acquainted with the Lord Jesus, we will have some very perceptible, godly characteristics to desire and to emulate. No doubt, yielding to the Holy Spirit's promptings should be our priority before we are open to appropriating this divine nature.

Point three: The powerful pronouncement that God's divine power has already been offered to all believers, including all things that pertain to both life and godliness, through the knowledge of Him who called us (v. 3). There are many other scriptural exhortations to simply be obedient to the changes for our maturity that our heavenly Father wants to bring about. Remember Jesus is the author and finisher of our faith, according to Hebrews 12:2. In fact, all of the New Testament is a clarion call to make discipleship our priority. A disciple is one who seeks, learns, and grows to become like his teacher.

Point four: We can be motivated by learning all the great and precious promises that are to be found in the New Testament. As we consider our lives to be like yielded clay in the care of the Master Potter, we will see changes. When we are obedient and don't resist His precise and unique, individualized molding, the outcome will be these very precious promises taking form and developing. We will become the new creatures in Christ that we were ordained to be!

Point five: A close look at verse four calls for a permanent position on our part. Peter writes that believers have escaped the corruption that is in the world. His implication is that we have escaped sin's power by choosing God's salvation and kingdom. We must realize that we have been enabled to resist the power of corruption and lust that exist in the world. It is by Christ's atoning sacrifice and by His Spirit now residing within us. It is folly to expect any part of His divine nature to come forth in a life that is giving place to the world's immorality and sinfulness.

The outline of the elements of change that are to be developed in us, as we yield to the ministry of God's Spirit, are presented in a connective manner in II Peter 1:5–7:

- giving all diligence, add to your faith virtue,
- to virtue knowledge,
- to knowledge self-control,
- to self-control perseverance,
- to perseverance godliness,
- to godliness brotherly kindness,
- and to brotherly kindness love.

These are the features of a developing disciple that are available to each of us. The outcome of diligently persevering in this radical personality change from the carnal, emotional person to the spiritually mature has numerous benefits. We are promised that we will be neither barren nor unfruitful in this present life (v. 8). Wouldn't the expression of these Christ-like qualities make dramatic changes in our everyday encounters and relationships?

We are assured that by making our calling and election sure through this disciplining program, we will not stumble (v. 10). As all believers easily recognize, when we stumble in our Christian walk, our witness is tarnished and we suffer disappointment and guilt that only asking for God's forgiveness can heal. In His mercy, He does this as often as is needed as part of our growth process.

Then we read of this wonderful future promise: "an entrance will be supplied to you abundantly into the everlasting kingdom of our Lord and Savior Jesus Christ" (v. 11). What a glorious motivation for being diligent in our growth process.

The divine nature is the legacy of God's Holy Spirit. It involves a growth process requiring the nourishment of the Spirit and the Word of God. Upon examination, we can see that this new nature is composed of attainable traits that we can rightfully seek to appropriate through an unflagging desire on our part.

Let us keep in mind that the Lord always desires the first fruits. As our roots go deeper into Him, we can present the first portion of the divine nature back to Him in loving, daily communion. He sees these characteristics as the normal result of our being "in Christ." He knows that the increased outflow of this new nature will be used to attract others to desire to be partakers of God's kingdom and the divine nature.

* * * * *

Prayer:

Dear heavenly Father: As I contemplate Your desire to work many needed changes in my life, I want to be yielded and pliable to those changes. Give me a greater understanding of Your new covenant. I want to be nourished by Your Word and Your Holy Spirit so I can receive the transformation of the divine nature that is in Jesus. It is in His name I ask. Amen.

CHAPTER 31

Appropriate Your Eternal Relationship

∞

Beloved, now we are children of God;
and it has not yet been revealed what we shall be,
but we know that when He is revealed,
we shall be like Him,
for we shall see Him as He is.
(I John 3:2)

Living in the light of our eternal relationship and destiny changes the very quality of our days. This is the manner in which we see Jesus living in the four gospels. He is always motivated by His eternal relationship to God the Father and also by the clear priorities of His purpose and destiny.

When we learn to live above the mundane, the weariness, and the frustrations that life brings, peace will be at the core of our existence. We can focus our attention on the marvelous knowledge that we have been invited into the eternal kingdom of our heavenly Father, the Creator of the whole universe!

"For our light affliction, which is but for a moment, is working for us a far more exceeding and eternal weight of glory" (II Corinthians 4:17).

As our fellowship with the Godhead grows more intimate and real, we will see His Spirit giving us scriptural revelations that take us from glory to glory. We will perceive the power of eternal life developing within us that cannot be shaken. The very fact that the Creator God calls us His children stirs an irrefutable awareness within that we have been invited into a timeless and divine family relationship.

One of the earliest Scripture records of the eternal God being called Father is as offerings were presented for the temple that King Solomon was to build. It presents us with a prayer of praise that still seems fitting as we also express thanksgiving for our eternal relationship: "and David said: 'Blessed are You, Lord God of Israel, our Father, forever and ever. Yours, O Lord, is the greatness, the power and the glory, the victory and the majesty; for all that is in heaven and in earth is Yours; Yours is the kingdom, O Lord, and You are exalted as head over all'" (I Chronicles 29:10–11).

We can appropriate and enlarge our understanding of this eternal relationship only as we seek the Lord and desire His Spirit to enlighten us. We often keep our attention so fixed on present circumstances that we fail to be fortified by who we really are. Those who meditate on the truth that today they are "in Christ" live in the present-day knowledge of their eternal relationship.

The blessed term "in Christ" is used numerous

times in the New Testament. Underline it when you read it and let it gain a deeper place in your understanding. Here is a great memory verse: "To them God willed to make known what are the riches of the glory of this mystery among the Gentiles: which is Christ *in you,* the hope of glory" (Colossians 1:27).

What joy we experience as we consider this large precious family we are a part of through the blood of Christ. Jesus said, "For whoever does the will of My Father in heaven is My brother and sister and mother" (Matthew 12:50). No one can say he is without family members and is alone in this world!

As we carry out our daily chores, we can keep in mind that our highest responsibility is to labor for eternal things that will not perish, but that Jesus said will endure to everlasting life (John 6:27). We have looked at many categories of being about our heavenly Father's business in these thirty-one chapters. We have learned that all believers have been provided with needed ministry giftings to serve the Lord in their unique world.

The very knowledge that God calls us His sons and daughters is ample motivation to be at His disposal, day by day. We grow as we serve Him. His Spirit is also encouraging us to exchange our carnal nature for the divine nature of His firstborn Son, Jesus the Christ. He is the anointed Messiah meant for all of mankind. He is the Savior of the world and King of Kings!

Remember this Christian life is "on-the-job training" for eternal responsibilities. "He who overcomes shall inherit all things, and I will be his God and he shall be My son" (Revelation 21:7). Let this sure promise of God take root in the center of your mind and heart.

The descriptions of our eternal destiny are of such lofty and superior dimensions that it is hard for our minds to grasp more than just the essence. But as one sage surmised, if we really understood what glories await us beyond this earthly realm, we would want to go there today! This must be why God in His great wisdom merely sprinkles the Bible with glimpses of eternity. He has so much for His children to attend to on earth while we are in preparation.

We can read a description of the new heaven and new earth in the last two chapters of the Bible. Chapters 21 and 22 of the book of Revelation give us all sorts of familiar items that we can relate to now. But our greatest heritage is the righteousness of Jesus Christ that will qualify and allow us to live in the presence of our heavenly Father and Jesus.

What a fine benediction to the reader as we come to the conclusion of this book—the clarion call and promise of Revelation 22:14 and 17: "Blessed are those who do His commandments, that they may have the right to the tree of life, and may enter through the gates into the city. . . . And the Spirit and the bride say, 'Come!' . . . Whoever desires, let him take the water of life freely."

* * * * *

Prayer:
Dear Father God: As I become more familiar with all of the dimensions of Your great love, and the careful provisions You have made for each of Your

family members, I thank You with all my heart that You have called me to also come. In the lovely name of my Savior, Lord, and King Jesus, I praise You now and forever. Amen.